THE EVERGREEN CLUB

COYOTE GRAY SR

Published by Coyote Pack Publishing

This is a work of fiction. All characters, including but not limited to the pineapple, the egg timer, the nugget ice, the labels, the puzzle, the raven, and the Armchair Psychoanalyst, are products of the author's imagination.

The dogs are based on real dogs. The dogs know who they are.

The pineapple is not a symbol of welcome.

Published in the United States of America

First Edition, 2026

ISBN: 978-1-972671-07-8

Library of Congress Cataloging in Publication Data has been applied for. The application did not explain itself. Neither did we. We consider this adequate.

Cover design by someone who was asked what the pineapple means and answered correctly.

Printed on paper that has been through things. The paper is fine. The paper does not wish to discuss it.

For my daughter-in-law, Margaret Gray,
who keeps the ranch and the kitchen running, and the quiet, steady,
and never asks for credit for either.

Few people know how to carry age properly.

Prologue

By the time you are old enough to be considered "seasoned," you discover that the world is run by people who believe seasoning is optional.

It is an odd moment, realizing you have become a historical artifact while still paying bills, still learning interfaces, still putting on shoes with the same grave attention previously reserved for courtrooms and wildlife. Youth has no training module for this. Youth offers practice in the beginning, not in the continuing. It rehearses appetite, not accounting.

So when you first receive an invitation to The Evergreen Club, you accept it the way you accept any invitation after sixty, which is to say you do not accept it at all until you have inspected the chairs.

The Evergreen Club does not list an address. It lists directions that read like advice from a person who has never been lost, never been found, and has strong opinions about both.

"Arrive when you are ready," it says. "The door will be open. The pineapple will not."

This is not explained. It is not even italicized, which implies institutional confidence.

The club exists in no particular decade. It is not antique. It is not modern. It is not retro. It simply refuses to participate in the question. The building looks as if it was designed by committee, then edited by someone who hated committees, then approved anyway because the forms were filed correctly and the committee had already moved on to parking.

Inside, the lighting is calm, the carpets are forgiving, and every surface is arranged with the sort of careful neutrality that suggests prior incidents. The room is not decorated. It is managed. Somewhere in its history, someone chose violence with a paint color, and the institution responded by choosing beige with the full weight of governance behind it.

On the central table, as promised, sits a single pineapple. Whole. Regal. Untouched. The fruit has the posture of a dignitary and the emotional warmth of a judge who has already decided the sentence but is letting you finish your statement out of professional courtesy. Nobody offers to cut it. Nobody asks why it is there. Nobody even looks at it for longer than politeness requires, long enough to confirm it is still winning.

To the left of the pineapple is an egg timer.

It rings.

Nobody jumps. Nobody asks what it means. Everyone nods solemnly, as if time itself has filed a motion and the motion has been granted without objection because objecting to time has never once worked, and everyone here knows it. Then a thin man in a tidy cardigan resets it without checking the dial. The new interval could be seven minutes. It could be a lifetime. It does not matter. The timer will ring when the timer rings, and the Club will continue to pretend this is both profound and orderly, because pretending things are orderly is how institutions survive, and pretending things are profound is how people do.

The host introduces himself as Austen.

This is not a surname, or at least not one he is using in public. He says it with a small, composed smile, like a person who has prepared for a certain kind of nonsense and is pleased to see it arrive on schedule. He is the kind of man who has never once raised his voice but has ended conversations simply by pausing long enough that the other person ran out of confidence.

"A seat," he says, gesturing to an armchair that looks both supportive and slightly judgmental, the way a good accountant looks at your receipts. "We try to avoid surprises. The furniture here is trained. We do not keep experimental chairs. We tried that once. The liability was philosophical."

I choose the chair that looks most like it has been through things and survived. It accepts me with the resigned patience of a structure that has heard every kind of person settle into it and has opinions about none of them, or possibly all of them, but has been trained not to say.

Austen glances at my shoes, my posture, my face, and my speed, in that order, and nods as if a private ledger has been updated. He does not write anything down. The ledger is internal. The ledger is always internal with people like Austen. The external version would be too honest for public use.

"You have brought your own gravity," he says approvingly. "That saves us time. We have had guests who arrive without any and spend the first hour borrowing everyone else's."

I have brought two dogs. Steinbeck is the steady one, a creature of simple agreements who has never met a floor he didn't trust and never met a person he didn't forgive. Hemingway is the one with opinions. He enters a room the way he enters all rooms, as if he has already formed a position on the furniture and is choosing not to share it yet, but will, and it will be brief, and he will consider the matter closed. Both of them look around the Club with the blunt confidence of beings who do not care whether anything here is tasteful as long as it is edible, and who have never once in their lives been troubled by the question of whether they belong somewhere, because the answer has always been yes and the question has always been someone else's problem.

An orange tabby cat arrives a moment later, not walking so much as appearing, the way cats do, with the smug certainty of a deity who has decided to visit the mortal world not out of love but out of boredom and a suspicion that someone somewhere is receiving attention that should be redirected. The cat is young, irritating, and convinced it is the first creature to have ever had an idea.

"Byron," Austen says, in the tone of a person naming a storm system that has already been downgraded once but refuses to behave like it.

Byron leaps onto the central table, circles the pineapple twice with the focused intensity of a creature performing a ritual it invented thirty seconds ago, and sits beside it like its deeply resentful personal assistant.

A black raven lands on the back of the sofa without asking permission and without making a sound that could be interpreted as a request. Nobody reacts. The bird folds itself into the room as if it has been here for decades, watching quietly, taking notes in a language no one else reads, waiting for something melodramatic to occur so it can pretend it predicted it and be technically correct, which is the only kind of correct that interests it.

"Poe," Austen says.

Poe blinks with mournful dignity and immediately begins studying the corners of the ceiling, as if hoping to find a tragedy someone forgot to clean up, or at minimum a cobweb with thematic potential.

On the far side of the room, a woman plugs something into the wall with brisk competence and no apology. A harsh fluorescent work light flares to life, flooding the snack table with the kind of brightness usually reserved for interrogations, autopsy suites, and the lighting department of a hardware store where all the employees have given up.

"I brought it to help everyone see the snacks better," she announces, smiling as if this is generosity and not an act of war against ambiance.

The snacks, now fully visible under what amounts to an industrial sun, look less like refreshments and more like evidence. A cracker display that had been perfectly respectable in soft light now looks like it was assembled during a hostage negotiation. A bowl of mixed nuts catches the glare and throws it back with the defiant energy of a thing that knows it was a last-minute purchase.

"That," Austen says, with the kind of effort that implies a long history of managing this exact situation, "is Woolf."

Woolf is already drifting through the room, moving items half an inch to the left, then pausing to stare into the middle distance with the intensity of someone listening to thoughts arrive by boat from a country that does not appear on any map but sends a great deal of mail. She seems to be conversing with an invisible committee, all of whom have opinions about napkins and none of whom agree, and all of whom she is quoting internally at a speed that makes her eyes move slightly, as if reading a transcript only she can see.

Behind Woolf, a man enters carrying a large box with the purposeful stride of someone who believes every room is improved by his arrival and every flat surface is a missed opportunity.

Without greeting, without preamble, without even the courtesy of eye contact, he dumps a thousand-piece puzzle onto the coffee table.

The pieces scatter like confetti at a funeral where nobody liked the deceased, but everyone agreed to attend because the catering was paid for.

He rubs his hands together with satisfaction and begins assembling the border with a confidence that suggests he believes the world still has edges, that those edges can be found, and that finding them is simply a matter of commitment and adequate table space.

"Dickens," Austen says, the way a firefighter says "structure fire," meaning the situation has a name, the name is accurate, and knowing the name does not make the situation smaller. "He cannot enter a room without immediately starting a project that involves everyone's surface area and at least two hours of someone else's evening."

Dickens looks up brightly. "It will be very satisfying once we find the corner pieces," he says, as though satisfaction is a guarantee and not a rumor started by optimists who have never attempted a puzzle with a solid blue sky.

A third guest arrives with a label maker slung over one shoulder like a sidearm. She moves toward the spice rack with the focused calm of a surgeon approaching a procedure she has performed so many times that her hands know the work before her mind authorizes it.

"I can label the host's spice rack," she says, scanning the room with the bright, acquisitive gaze of a person who sees disorder everywhere and considers herself the cure. "I can label the guests' drinks. I can label the guests. I can label the furniture. I can label the labels."

"No," Austen says, with the practiced firmness of someone who has had this conversation before and knows it will not end but can at least be managed. "We have tried that. The results were bureaucratic."

"Twain," he adds, softer, the way one names a condition that is chronic but not fatal.

Twain grins, the grin of a person who has already won because the label maker is loaded and resistance only delays the inevitable. "It saves conversation," she says, and begins printing labels anyway, because Twain has never once in her life accepted a boundary she did not first test, label, and file.

Another guest enters carrying a bag of nugget ice as if it contains the last uncontaminated resource on an otherwise compromised planet.

"This is the good ice," he says, holding it up for inspection with the gravity of a man presenting evidence to a jury he already knows is against him.

"We have ice," Austen says.

"Yes," the man replies, pitying him with the full depth of a pity that has been refined over years of watching people settle for inferior ice, "but you do not have the good ice. You have ice that was made by a machine that does not understand its purpose. This ice," and here he pauses, because the moment requires it, "this ice was made by a machine that understands."

He will not be reasoned with. He will not use the host's freezer ice. He will not entertain the notion that ice is ice. His loyalty is not to water in its general frozen state but to a particular texture of water, a particular density, a particular chew, acquired from a specific fast food chain at a specific location and guarded with the seriousness of a man who has found the one thing in the world that is exactly right and will not be told it doesn't matter.

"Melville," Austen says to me, barely above a whisper, as if naming him any louder might set off the full lecture. "Obsessed with a thing. Entirely sincere. Not negotiable. The ice is his whale. Do not ask him about it unless you have cleared your afternoon and made peace with your choices."

Melville places the bag carefully on the table near the pineapple, adjusting its position twice, as if arranging an altar that must face a direction only he can calculate. Byron the cat sniffs the bag, recoils, and looks offended that something in the room is receiving attention and it is not about him.

The egg timer rings again.

The room nods.

Austen resets it.

No one asks. Everyone understands, which is to say no one understands, and it would be impolite to admit it; impoliteness is the one thing the Evergreen Club does not permit, not because it values manners, but because it values the particular kind of silence that manners make possible.

Then the Armchair Psychoanalyst arrives.

He is not introduced because he introduces himself, and he introduces himself by studying you for three seconds with the penetrating focus of a man who took one psychology course in 1974 and has been dining out on it ever since, and then explaining your childhood.

"Interesting," he says, not as a compliment, not as an observation, but as a diagnosis delivered with the warmth of a man who believes that understanding people is the same as helping them. "You carry your history in your shoulders."

"I carry my history in my calendar," I say. "The shoulders are just along for the ride."

He laughs the way a therapist laughs, which is to say he does not laugh; he processes your humor and returns it to you with annotations. "Deflection," he says warmly. "Classic. You use humor to keep people from noticing your fear of decline."

"I use humor to keep people from noticing my fear of this conversation."

He smiles, delighted. Everything you say is evidence. Every sentence is a specimen. He is the only person in the room who is having a good time, and his good time depends entirely on your discomfort, which he would call "progress" and which you would call "Wednesday."

I have met this guest before in many forms. He arrives at every gathering where people over sixty are present, sometimes as a fellow guest, sometimes as a relative, sometimes as a medical professional who has confused proximity with permission. He does not converse. He extracts. He takes normal sentences and treats them like clues from a crime scene. He turns a casual observation about crackers into an intervention. He cannot hear someone say "I'm tired" without asking what they're really tired of.

"Who invited him?" I ask Austen.

"He invited himself," Austen says, with the resignation

of a man who has tried every available method of un-inviting someone and discovered that the Psychoanalyst interprets exclusion as confirmation of his importance. "He believes all gatherings are cries for help. He considers his presence the answer."

The Psychoanalyst sits in the most comfortable chair without asking, without hesitation, and without the faintest awareness that choosing the best seat in a room full of older people is itself a diagnostic act. This is his first official move.

He looks at my dogs. "Ah," he says, with the satisfaction of a man finding exactly what he expected to find. "Companionship as emotional regulation. The steady one is your anchor. The opinionated one is the self you do not permit in public."

Steinbeck wags his tail because someone is talking, and talking sometimes means food.

Hemingway stares at the Psychoanalyst with the flat, unblinking assessment of a dog who has just decided something about a person and will not be updating his file.

The Psychoanalyst looks at Byron. "Youth," he says, "is a performance of invincibility staged for an audience that has already left."

Byron yawns with theatrical boredom and bats a puzzle piece off the table. It lands near Poe, who ignores it.

He looks at Poe. "And you," he says softly, leaning forward, "are a messenger."

Poe stares at him with the calm contempt of a creature who has watched humans turn meaning into theater for so many centuries that the performance no longer registers as interesting. The raven cocks its head, as if considering whether to correct him, then decides to let him be wrong because it is funnier, and because being wrong with confidence is the most human thing Poe has ever witnessed, and at this point, the bird finds it almost endearing.

The Psychoanalyst turns his attention back to me with the smooth pivot of a man who believes every conversation is about him, even when he is asking about you.

"Tell us," he says, as if the room has agreed to a group exercise nobody remembers signing up for, "about your health. Your problems. Your surgeries. Your medicines. Your procedures. Your body's ongoing negotiation with gravity."

This is the moment. The opening of the trap. The oldest trap in every room where the median age exceeds the speed limit. There are two correct ways to respond to this question after sixty.

One is to refuse.

The other is to answer briefly, intending to say a single sentence, and then accidentally talk for forty minutes because the body after sixty is a filing cabinet and once you open one drawer, the adjacent drawers start sliding out on their own, and before you know it, you are describing a knee replacement to someone who asked about your weekend.

The room is full of older people, which means the room is full of inventories. An older body is not a body. It is a ledger. It is an annotated record of repairs, compromises, and renegotiated terms. It is a living list of parts that once operated silently and now require meetings. But the Evergreen Club is designed, by Austen's careful architecture, to prevent the gathering from becoming a competitive medical recital, the way many respectable evenings have been destroyed by the phrase, "So they put a stent in," followed by three hours of counteroffers.

Austen glances at the pineapple.

The pineapple does nothing. The pineapple has never done anything. The pineapple's entire contribution to the Club is its refusal to participate, which makes it the most effective member.

The egg timer rings.

Austen resets it with calm violence, a phrase that should not make sense but does if you have ever watched a person perform a small mechanical action while containing a large emotional response.

Woolf begins humming something that might be a hymn or might be an argument she is having with a memory. "Finals," she murmurs, as if that explains everything, and it does, if you understand that for Woolf every moment is a final examination in a subject she did not know she was enrolled in.

Dickens searches the puzzle pieces with growing intensity, his fingers moving across the table like a man reading braille written by an enemy. He has found fourteen edge pieces and no corners. He treats this as a temporary setback. He will treat it as a temporary setback for the rest of the evening, and possibly the rest of his life.

Twain approaches the Psychoanalyst with a strip of labels and an expression that combines hospitality with the energy of a person who has been waiting for this specific opportunity since she arrived.

"Would you like your drink labeled," she asks, "or would you prefer we label you directly? I can do either. I can do both. I have supplies."

The Psychoanalyst smiles indulgently, as if your behavior is a gift he is unwrapping for educational purposes. "A need for control," he says. "Labeling is how you manage uncertainty. It is how you create the illusion of order in a world that refuses to hold still."

"Close," Twain replies, and sticks a label onto his lapel anyway.

It reads: PROVISIONAL.

He looks down at it. He does not remove it. He cannot remove it without acknowledging it bothers him, and acknowledging something bothers him would require the kind of self-awareness he has spent decades redirecting toward other people. The label stays. Twain has won, and she has won in the way she always wins, which is quickly, quietly, and with adhesive.

Melville guards the nugget ice with grim devotion, occasionally lifting the bag to check its structural integrity the way a new parent checks a sleeping child, not because anything has changed but because vigilance is a form of love and he will not be caught unprepared by condensation.

Byron climbs onto my lap, kneads once with claws that are sharper than the situation requires, then bites me gently on the hand, as if to remind me that youth is mostly enthusiasm without policy, energy without memory, confidence without the experience to know what confidence costs. It is annoying in the way youth always is, and in the way youth always stops being, if it survives long enough to learn that the world bites back and does not do it gently.

Poe fluffs his feathers and emits a single sound that is not quite a caw, not quite a sigh, not quite a judgment, and not quite a benediction, but occupies the exact space where all four overlap.

I look around the room.

At the pineapple, holding court from the center of the table with the serene authority of a fruit that has outlasted every conversation ever held in its presence. At the timer, which measures nothing and means everything. At Woolf's light, bleaching the snacks into the kind of visibility that makes you wish for darkness. At the puzzle that will outlast the evening, the month, and possibly Western civilization. At the labels being applied to objects that did not request identity and will not benefit from it, but will wear it anyway, because Twain does not accept refusals. At the bag of good ice being guarded like a reliquary by a man whose devotion to frozen water has reached a purity that most religions would envy. At the Psychoanalyst, who will never be fully right but will always be almost right, which is the most tiring kind of wrong there is, because you cannot dismiss it, you cannot accept it, and you cannot escape it without leaving the room, and leaving the room would only prove his point.

And I understand what the invitation was actually offering.

Not a club. Not a gathering. Not a social event, a support group, or a program with measurable outcomes and a newsletter.

A rehearsal.

A place where time is acknowledged without being worshiped. Where decline is permitted to exist in the room without becoming the room's only subject. Where the old can be strange, particular, obsessive, and unreasonable without being treated as tragic. Where a man can guard a bag of ice without anyone trying to fix him. Where a woman can label the world without anyone asking her to stop, except Austen, who asks her to stop exactly once per evening as a formality they both respect. Where a puzzle can go unfinished, and this is not a failure. Where a pineapple can sit at the center of everything and explain nothing, and this is not a problem but a principle.

A place where the young, represented by an orange bitey cat with no sense of proportion, can be tolerated as a temporary weather system that will eventually learn what the rest of the room already knows, which is that the weather always passes and the room remains.

Austen returns to my chair with a small notepad and a pen that looks like it has signed things that mattered.

"We have a matter to discuss," he says. "A practical matter. A matter of governance."

He says the last word the way a man says "plumbing," meaning there will be no glamour and no one will enjoy it, but it must be handled correctly or the house will fill with water, and the water will not care about your feelings.

He sits across from me, pen poised, back straight, with the posture of a man who has spent his entire life believing that how you sit in a chair communicates more than anything you could say from it.

"The Evergreen Club," he says, "has been asked to take responsibility for something it did not create, does not want, and cannot refuse without consequences that would be worse than acceptance."

Poe leans forward on the sofa back, feathers tightening, as if the air has just become worth paying attention to.

Byron stops biting my hand, briefly, which for Byron constitutes a standing ovation.

Steinbeck sighs the sigh of a dog who has heard serious tones before and knows they usually mean someone is about to rearrange the furniture.

Hemingway does not move. Hemingway decided his position when he entered the room and saw no reason to update it based on new information.

The egg timer rings.

Austen does not reset it this time.

The silence after the ring is different from all the silences before it. Every previous ring was a ritual. This one is a punctuation mark. The timer has stopped being a prop and become a clock, and clocks, unlike timers, do not reset. Clocks only go forward. Everyone in the room knows this. Everyone in the room has known this for a long time. This is, after all, what the room is for.

Austen looks at me, calm and direct, with the expression of a man who is about to ask you for something he already knows you will agree to, not because he has manipulated you but because he has accurately assessed that you are the kind of person who agrees to things like this, and he respects you enough to let you pretend you had a choice.

"It has been decided," he says, "that you are the only person in this room who can keep the pineapple from becoming policy."

He pauses.

"There are people coming," he says. "People with plans. People who believe that what we do here should have a name, a mission, a structure, and a brochure. People who believe the pineapple should mean something official."

He sets down the pen.

"Your job," he says, "is to make sure it doesn't."

PRIVATE LEDGER ENTRY:

I brought the dogs. Steinbeck already trusts the floor. Hemingway is still deciding if the pineapple is an enemy or just furniture. Austen looked at my shoes first, then my face. I looked at the timer. Neither of us said what we both saw: the room is already keeping score.

Chapter 1

THE SITUATION ROOM

The letter arrived on a Tuesday, which is the day most institutional threats arrive because Monday is reserved for recovering from the weekend, Wednesday is too central to the week to tolerate disruption, Thursday is already committed to anticipating Friday, and Friday itself has diplomatic immunity. Tuesday is the day the world sends its formal notices, its jury summonses, its termination letters, and its invitations to strategic visioning sessions, because Tuesday has no defenders and no allies and will accept whatever is placed upon it without complaint.

Austen held the letter with two fingers, the way a person holds a document that is not yet dangerous but has the structural potential to become so, the way a demolitions expert holds a device that has not been armed but is built to be armed, and treating it casually would be a professional failure even if treating it seriously turns out to have been unnecessary.

"We have received correspondence," he said.

He said "correspondence" the way other people say

"diagnosis." The word entered the room, and the room adjusted. Dickens stopped working on the puzzle, which was remarkable because he had not stopped since the evening he brought it, and the border was now complete, but the interior remained a vast, unsorted democracy of blue sky and what appeared to be a barn. Twain set down her label maker, which was the equivalent of a gunslinger holstering a weapon, not because the threat had passed but because the situation required both hands free. Woolf turned from the window where she had been studying a pattern of light on the far wall that she would later describe as "the exact color of an unfinished thought." Melville tightened his grip on the bag of nugget ice, which had been replaced since the last meeting with a fresh bag from the same specific location because Melville did not trust ice that had been frozen for more than seventy-two hours, a position he had defended at length on more than one occasion and which no one had the stamina to challenge again.

The Psychoanalyst, who had been analyzing the posture of a floor lamp, turned with the eager focus of a man who has just been told that a group crisis is developing and considers this excellent news.

I was in my chair. The chair that had been through things. Steinbeck was at my feet, steady as a dock, the kind of dog who responds to tension by becoming more horizontal, as if his contribution to any emergency is to demonstrate that the floor is still available and the floor has never once overreacted to anything. Hemingway was across the room, standing, because Hemingway did not sit down during announcements. He had positioned himself near the door, not because he intended to leave but because he believed in options, and a dog who stands near the door during a crisis is a dog who has thought about logistics, even if his plan begins and ends with the door.

Byron was on the table, sitting on three puzzle pieces and a napkin, watching the room with the alert disinterest of a creature who senses that something important is happening to other people and is calculating how to make it about himself.

Poe was on the curtain rod. Poe was always on the curtain rod during formal proceedings, the way a judge is always on the bench, not because the position is comfortable, but because it is correct.

"The letter," Austen continued, "is from the Department of Community Enrichment and Senior Engagement."

He paused to let the name do its work.

It did its work.

The Department of Community Enrichment and Senior Engagement is the kind of name that is produced when a committee is asked to create something that sounds supportive, and instead creates something that sounds like a diagnosis delivered by a building. Every word in the name is individually harmless. Together, they form a bureaucratic compound that suggests someone, somewhere, has decided that a group of older people is not enriched enough or engaged enough, and that both failures can be corrected through departmental intervention.

"Senior," Twain repeated, tasting the word the way a person tastes something that might have turned. "They used the word 'senior.'"

"They did."

"In reference to us."

"In reference to this Club and its members, yes."

Twain reached for the label maker. The holstering had

been premature. "I would like to label that word," she said, "and I would like the label to be comprehensive."

"You may label it later," Austen said. "First, I will read the letter."

He unfolded it with the care of a man disarming something. The paper was thick, official, the kind of paper that believes its own weight constitutes authority. It had a letterhead that included a logo, and the logo included a tree, and the tree was the kind of tree that appears on institutional stationery when the institution wants to communicate growth, stability, and the passage of time without actually committing to any of those things. It was a tree designed by someone who had once seen a tree and remembered the general concept but not the details, so it looked like a tree, the way a scarecrow looks like a farmer.

Austen read:

"Dear Members of the Evergreen Club. It has come to the attention of the Department of Community Enrichment and Senior Engagement that your organization has been meeting regularly at the above address without formal registration, programming oversight, or liability documentation. We applaud your initiative."

He paused. "They applaud our initiative."

"Generous," I said.

"Magnanimous," Austen agreed, in the tone of a man accepting a compliment from someone who has just broken into his house. He continued reading.

"As part of our ongoing commitment to supporting vibrant community spaces for older adults, we would like to propose a strategic visioning session to explore how the Department might assist in formalizing your activities, expanding your programming, and ensuring your organization meets current standards for community based senior engagement. We believe that with proper support, the Ever-green Club could become a model for intergenerational enrichment in the greater community."

Austen folded the letter.

The room was silent in the way rooms are after a deto-nation, not because there was nothing to say, but because the debris was still settling, and speaking too soon risked inhaling something.

"Vibrant," Twain said. She had begun printing a label before the word finished leaving her mouth. The label read: THREAT LEVEL: VIBRANT.

"They want to formalize our activities," Dickens said, leaning forward with the expression of a man who has been told a new project exists and is already mentally staffing it. "Well. That is not unreasonable. We could form a small committee to review the proposal, draft a preliminary response, establish terms of engagement, and create a subcommittee to oversee the committee's findings. I can have a framework by Thursday."

"Dickens," Austen said.

"Wednesday evening, if I skip the puzzle."

"Dickens."

"I am only saying that if they want structure, we should be the ones to provide it. We should meet their structure with a superior structure. We should out organize them. I will need a whiteboard. I will need two whiteboards. And possibly a third whiteboard to coordinate the first two."

"Dickens. No."

Dickens sat back, wounded but not defeated. Dickens was never defeated. Dickens was only between projects.

Woolf, who had been standing near the snack table with her fluorescent light unplugged since the events of the previous month, spoke without turning around. "The letter assumes we are incomplete," she said. Her voice was distant, as if she were narrating from inside a room adjacent to this one, a room that contained the same furniture but different light. "It reads us the way a doctor reads a chart. It sees symptoms where we see the constitution. The department does not know that we are not broken. The department assumes all rooms without paperwork are rooms that have not yet been fixed."

She turned. "I do not wish to be fixed," she said. "I was not aware I required it."

The room absorbed this.

Melville lifted his bag of ice. "The real question," he said, with the certainty of a man who has carried a single thesis through every conversation he has ever entered, "is whether they understand the ice situation."

"There is no ice situation," Austen said, which was a sentence Austen had said so many times it had become a kind of liturgical response, the way a congregation says "and also with you," not because it means anything fresh but because the rhythm requires it.

"There is always an ice situation," Melville replied. "The ice situation is the foundational situation. Every other situation sits on top of it. You do not build a house without a foundation. You do not run a club without the right ice. If this department wants to come in here and reorganize things, the first thing they will do is replace the ice. They will bring institutional ice. Commissary ice. Ice made by a machine that reports to a budget committee. Ice that has been frozen according to policy. And that," he said, raising one finger with the solemnity of a man delivering a prophecy he expects will be ignored, "is when we will have truly lost."

Nobody argued with Melville about the ice. Arguing

with Melville about the ice was like arguing with the weather. The weather does not hear you. The weather is not interested in your position. The weather will continue regardless, and the only thing your argument accomplishes is making you wet.

The Psychoanalyst, who had been listening with the bright, collecting expression of a man at a buffet, leaned forward. He had not yet been asked to speak. He never waited to be asked. Being asked implied that his contribution was optional, and he had never once considered his contribution optional.

"This is a fascinating moment," he said. "The group is being asked to confront its relationship with authority. The letter represents the parental structure. The Club represents the autonomous self. The tension between them is the tension of individuation."

"The tension," I said, "is that someone wants to give us a brochure."

"Yes," the Psychoanalyst said, undeterred, because the Psychoanalyst was never deterred by disagreement, only nourished by it. "And the brochure is the mechanism of control. It names you. It defines you. It tells you what you are before you have decided for yourself. You resist the brochure because you resist being narrated by an external authority."

"I resist the brochure because it will use the word 'vibrant,'" I said.

"There," he said, pointing at me with the satisfied expression of a man who has just confirmed his own theory using the other person's denial as evidence. "Humor as deflection. You mock the word to avoid engaging with the feeling."

"I mock the word because it deserves it."

"And the mocking protects you from what?"

"From the word 'vibrant.'"

The Psychoanalyst nodded slowly, the nod of a man who has decided that your resistance is the most interesting thing about you, and he could do this all day, and he would, and he was, and there was no exit from the loop except silence or leaving the room, and leaving the room would only prove his point, which meant silence was the only option, which he would also interpret as significant, which meant there was no option at all, which is the fundamental experience of being in a room with a person who has decided that everything you do is data.

Hemingway walked over to the Psychoanalyst's chair and sat on his foot.

The Psychoanalyst looked down. "Ah," he said. "The dog as proxy. Expressing what the owner cannot."

Hemingway was not expressing anything. Hemingway had simply decided that the Psychoanalyst's foot was in a location that Hemingway preferred to occupy, and Hemingway operated on the principle that any space could be claimed by sitting on it, and the previous occupant's feelings about this were not part of the calculation. This was not a proxy expression. This was real estate.

"We need a response," Austen said, steering the room back toward the operational. Austen always steered the room back toward the operational. It was his primary function, the way a rudder's primary function is not to be interesting but to prevent the entire vessel from turning in circles, which is what the vessel would do if left to the conversational currents of its passengers.

"A letter," he said. "A formal response. Measured. Polite. Firm. It must acknowledge receipt without acknowledging authority. It must express gratitude without expressing submission. It must decline the visioning session without creating the impression that we have something to hide, because we do not have something to hide, we have something to protect, and the difference between hiding and protecting is the difference between guilt and sovereignty, and if we get the tone wrong, they will interpret protection as hiding and arrive with clipboards."

He looked at me.

Everyone looked at me.

This is what happens when you are the person in a room who has been identified as the one who works with words. It is a designation that, once assigned, cannot be returned, like a library book that the system has permanently checked out to your name, even after you have placed it back on the shelf. You become the person who drafts things. The person who can, presumably, find the exact arrangement of language that says "no" while sounding like "thank you" while meaning "never" while reading like "perhaps." You are expected to perform this trick not because it is easy, but because everyone else has decided it is your particular talent, the way Melville's talent is ice, Twain's talent is labels, and Dickens's talent is creating organizational structures that reproduce faster than the problems they were designed to solve.

"I will draft something," I said.

"It should be brief," Austen said.

"It will be brief."

"It should not be funny."

"I make no promises."

"It should not mention the pineapple."

I looked at the pineapple. The pineapple sat in the center of the table with the same immovable authority it had always possessed, the authority of a thing that has never explained itself and has never needed to. Byron was sitting next to it, one paw resting on its crown, as if claiming it. The cat looked like a tiny dictator posing with a national monument.

"The pineapple," I said, "is not mentioned in the letter."

"The pineapple," Austen said, "is the reason for the letter. It may not be named. But it is the reason. Somewhere, someone saw this Club, saw this room, saw this pineapple sitting on this table surrounded by people who could not explain it, and decided that anything unexplained must be unmanaged, and anything unmanaged must be assisted, and anything assisted must be documented, and once it is documented, it is theirs."

He straightened the pineapple by a quarter inch. It did not need straightening. The straightening was not for the pineapple.

"The pineapple," he said, "stays off the record. If the pineapple enters the official correspondence, the pineapple becomes subject to interpretation, and once it is subject to interpretation it will be interpreted, and once it is interpreted it will be redefined, and once it is redefined it will be put on a brochure, and the brochure will call it a symbol of welcome, and it is not a symbol of welcome. It is a pineapple. It is our pineapple. And it does not welcome. It presides."

Byron meowed, which was not agreement but was timed well enough to function as agreement, which is the cat's primary contribution to any serious discussion.

"I will write the letter tonight," I said. "Hemingway will supervise."

Hemingway, still sitting on the Psychoanalyst's foot, did not look up. Hemingway's editorial method was to be present and unimpressed until the work was finished, at which point he would walk away, which meant either approval or indifference, and the distinction was not available for clarification.

Steinbeck wagged his tail. Steinbeck's editorial method was to support all efforts unconditionally and then fall asleep.

Dickens was already sketching something on a napkin. "I have some thoughts on structure," he said. "The response should have an introduction, a body, a counterproposal, three appendices, and a timeline."

"It should have four sentences," Austen said.

"Four sentences cannot hold a counterproposal."

"Four sentences will not need one."

Dickens looked at his napkin. The napkin already had six paragraphs on it. He folded it carefully and placed it in his pocket, where it would join the other napkins, the growing archive of plans that had been drafted, deferred, and preserved because Dickens could not bear to discard a structure, even a failed one, even a rejected one, because every structure was a child and every child deserved a drawer.

Twain had finished her labels. She approached the letter on the table and placed one directly on the envelope.

It read: RECEIVED. NOT ACCEPTED. CONTENTS UNDER REVIEW. VIBRANT STATUS: DENIED.

It was the most labels she had ever used on a single object. This was, for Twain, the equivalent of shouting.

Woolf drifted toward the door, paused, and said, without looking at anyone, "They will come whether we write back or not. The letter is not a question. It is a notification. They have already decided. They are waiting for us to agree with what they have already done."

She left the room, taking the fluorescent light with her, then returning it, then standing in the doorway holding it as if she could not decide whether the light belonged inside the room where the problem was or outside the room where the problem was not yet visible, and the choice between those two locations was the choice between confrontation and preparation, and she was not ready to commit to either.

She put the light down by the door. This was a compromise. Woolf's compromises always involved placing an object in a transitional space and letting the object decide.

Melville was filling glasses with nugget ice. He did this during moments of crisis, the way other people make tea. The ice was comfort. The ice was certainty. The ice was the one thing in the room that was exactly what it claimed to be.

He handed me a glass.

"Good ice," he said.

I drank. The ice was, I had to admit, very good. It had the yielding crunch of something that had been frozen at exactly the right temperature by a machine that, as Melville insisted, understood its purpose. Whether a machine could understand its purpose was a philosophical question that Melville had answered for himself and saw no need to revisit.

The egg timer rang.

Austen looked at it for a long moment. Longer than usual. The timer sat next to the pineapple, which sat next to Byron, who sat next to Poe's shadow on the table, cast from the curtain rod above. The arrangement looked like a still life painted by someone with strong opinions about governance.

Austen reset the timer.

The interval began again.

The Club was still here. The letter was on the table. The response was unwritten. The pineapple was unexplained. The ice was good. The puzzle was unsolved. The labels were multiplying. The Psychoanalyst's foot was occupied.

And somewhere, in an office with its own fluorescent lighting and its own tree logo and its own vocabulary of words like "vibrant" and "engagement" and "strategic visioning," someone was waiting for a reply that would tell them everything they needed to know about a room they had never been in and a pineapple they would never understand.

I went home and wrote the letter.

It was four sentences long.

It did not mention the pineapple.

Hemingway supervised from across the room, unimpressed but present, which was all the editorial oversight the letter required, and more than most letters ever receive, and exactly enough.

Chapter 2

FIRST CONTACT

Shelley arrived on a Thursday, which should have been safe. Thursday is the day that has already survived the week and is coasting toward Friday on institutional momentum. Thursday does not invite conflict. Thursday is the day you schedule things you expect to go smoothly because the week has used up its capacity for disruption, and everyone involved has settled into the low, agreeable hum of people who have decided to postpone their problems until Monday.

But Shelley did not arrive the way problems arrive. She arrived the way the weather arrives when the forecast said clear skies, and you left your windows open.

She was younger than I expected. Not young in the way Byron is young. She was young in the way that institutions produce young people, and her training had prepared her for whatever she was about to encounter. She wore a lanyard. The lanyard carried an ID badge with her photograph and title, Community Enrichment Liaison, which means a person has been sent to enrich you, whether you have requested it or not. She carried a leather portfolio that was too nice for the job, suggesting either personal investment in the work or a gift from someone who believed it was important, and either possibility made her more difficult to dismiss than she would have been with a cheaper folder.

She also carried a tote bag. The tote bag said BUILDING BRIDGES, BUILDING COMMUNITY in a font that implied both the building and the bridges were metaphorical, which is the kind of font that is designed by people who believe metaphors are load bearing.

Austen opened the door before she knocked, because Austen always opened the door before visitors knocked. This was not prescience. This was logistics. Austen monitored the front walk the way a lighthouse monitors the coast, not because every approaching vessel is a threat, but because an unmonitored approach is undignified, and Austen believed that the first three seconds of any encounter established the terms for everything that followed. If you opened the door before the knock, you were the one granting entry. If you waited for the knock, you were the one responding to a request. The difference was small, procedural, and, to Austen, everything.

"You must be from the Department," Austen said, in the same tone a person uses when identifying a species of weather they have been tracking on the radar.

"I'm Shelley," she said, and smiled.

The smile was the problem.

It was not a bureaucratic smile. It was not the smile of a person executing a task. It was genuine. It was warm. It was the smile of a person who had entered a building she fully believed she was going to help, and the belief was not cynical, and the warmth was not performed and the help was not contingent on anything except her own conviction that helping was what she was here to do. She was not an adversary. She was a believer. And believers are harder to resist than adversaries because adversaries you can outmaneuver, but believers you can only disappoint, and disappointing a believer feels like kicking a dog, which is something nobody in this room would ever do, not even to a metaphorical dog, and especially not with Steinbeck and Hemingway present as character witnesses.

"Please come in," Austen said, and the invitation cost him something. You could see it in the quarter-second delay between the decision and the words, the brief internal negotiation between hospitality and self preservation that Austen resolved, as he always resolved things, in favor of the form. You invite people in. You offer them a seat. You behave as though the situation is manageable even when you suspect it is not, because the alternative is to behave as though it is not, and that concedes the first three seconds.

Shelley entered the Club the way a naturalist enters a habitat: observing everything, touching nothing, cataloguing with her eyes while her hands stayed politely at her sides. She took in the carpets, the furniture, the careful neutrality of the walls, the lighting that Woolf had left unplugged since the previous meeting, the puzzle that Dickens had expanded by fourteen pieces in the last week and which now included what appeared to be a portion of sky and one definitive corner, which Dickens had celebrated with the restrained joy of a man who has been vindicated by geometry.

She saw the snack table, which today featured crackers, a cheese plate of moderate ambition, and a bowl of mixed nuts that had been refreshed since the last meeting but still carried the general energy of a thing that exists because someone felt obligated to provide it.

She saw Twain's labels. There were more of them now. The spice rack had been labeled during a previous session despite Austen's prohibition, and each label was technically accurate but written with a specificity that crossed the line from identification into commentary. The oregano was labeled OREGANO (ADEQUATE). The paprika was labeled PAPRIKA (ASPIRATIONAL). The cinnamon was labeled CINNAMON (OVERPERFORMING). Twain had also labeled the label maker itself. The label read: ESSENTIAL PERSONNEL.

Shelley looked at the labels for a long time. She took out a small notebook and wrote something down. This was the first note she took. It would not be the last. Shelley took notes the way some people take photographs, compulsively, as if the act of recording a thing was the same as understanding it, and the notebook was not a tool but a companion, a second brain that she trusted more than the first because the second brain did not forget and did not editorialize and did not wake up at three in the morning wondering if it had misread the room.

She saw Melville's ice station. Since the letter arrived, Melville had upgraded his setup. The bag of nugget ice now sat in a small insulated cooler he had purchased specifically for the purpose of maintaining optimal temperature during what he called "extended operational periods," by which he meant meetings that lasted more than an hour, by which he meant every meeting, because no meeting at the Evergreen Club had ever lasted less than an hour and most of them lasted until Austen reset the egg timer for the final time and said "same time next week" in a tone that was both a dismissal and a benediction.

She saw the egg timer.

She saw the pineapple.

She paused at the pineapple.

Everyone in the room watched her pause at the pineapple. It was a particular kind of watching, the watching of people who are waiting to see if a newcomer will ask the question, because the question is the test and the answer to the test is that there is no answer and the correct response to the absence of an answer is to accept it, and accepting the absence of an answer to a visible, obvious, unexplained pineapple sitting in the center of an otherwise orderly room is the thing that separates people who belong in the Club from people who do not.

"What," Shelley said, and here she did the thing, the precise thing, the thing that everyone was waiting for her to do, "is the pineapple for?"

The room held its breath. Not dramatically. Not the way rooms hold their breath in novels where someone is about to reveal a secret. The room held its breath the way a room full of older people holds its breath when a younger person asks a question that reveals, in five words, the precise nature of the gap between them.

Austen looked at the pineapple. The pineapple looked at nothing, because it was a pineapple. But it looked at nothing with the authority of a thing that has chosen not to look at something, which is different from not having anything to look at.

"It is a pineapple," Austen said.

This was the complete answer. It was also the correct answer. It was not a satisfying answer, which is what made it correct, because the Club was built on the principle that not everything needs to be satisfying to be true, and the compulsion to make everything satisfying is the compulsion that leads to brochures.

"Yes," Shelley said, and smiled again, the patient smile of a person who has been trained in active listening and believes that if she waits long enough, the real answer will arrive behind the first one. "But what does it represent? Is it a tradition? A symbol? Part of your programming?"

"We do not have programming," Austen said.

"Part of your activities, then."

"It is not an activity. It is a pineapple."

"It's decorative?"

"It is not decorative. Decorative implies intention toward aesthetic effect. The pineapple does not intend. It presides."

Shelley wrote this down. She wrote down "pineapple presides." I could see the words from my chair because she wrote in the large, clear handwriting of a person who has been trained to take notes that other people will need to read later, which meant these notes were not private. These notes were institutional. These notes would be filed.

The pineapple had entered the record.

I looked at Austen. Austen's face did not change, but something behind his face changed, the way the sky does not change color when a storm is approaching from the wrong side but the light shifts and you know because you have lived under that sky long enough to recognize the difference between light that is calm and light that is calm because it has not yet been told what is coming.

Shelley moved through the room with professional warmth, greeting each member individually, and each member responded in the manner their character demanded.

Dickens stood, shook her hand, and immediately began describing the puzzle. "It is a thousand pieces," he said. "We are approximately four percent complete. The remaining ninety-six percent is a matter of dedication and surface area. Would you like to find an edge piece? Everyone should contribute. Contribution builds community." He said the last sentence without irony, because Dickens did not have irony. Dickens had enthusiasm, which was better armor and worse company.

Shelley found an edge piece within thirty seconds. Dickens was delighted. "You see?" he said to the room, as if the discovery of a single edge piece by a guest had validated his entire philosophy. "Engagement. Participation. Progress." He said these words the way Shelley's department said them, but he meant them differently, the way two people can use the word "love" to describe entirely different conditions.

Twain approached Shelley before Shelley could approach Twain, which was a tactical decision. Twain preferred to be the one initiating contact because it meant she controlled the terms, and controlling the terms meant she could label them.

"Would you like a name tag?" Twain asked.

"Oh, I have one," Shelley said, touching her lanyard.

"Not an institutional one. A real one." Twain held up the label maker with the patient confidence of a person offering salvation to someone who does not yet know they need it. "I can customize it. Font. Border. Subtitle."

"Subtitle?"

"Some members have subtitles. Melville's says ICE AUTHORITY. Dickens says PROJECT MANAGER (UNSANCTIONED). The pineapple has one, but I'm not allowed to apply it."

"What does it say?"

"MANAGEMENT."

Shelley laughed. She laughed the way a person laughs when they believe something is charming and quirky and have not yet considered the possibility that it is structural and serious.

"I'll just use my lanyard for now," Shelley said.

"The offer stands," Twain said, in the tone of a person who knows you will come around because everyone comes around because the labels are inevitable, and resistance is a label in itself.

Woolf did not approach Shelley. Woolf was approached. This was how Woolf operated. She did not initiate social contact. She existed in a space, and eventually the space delivered people to her, the way a river delivers things to a bend without the bend needing to reach for them.

Shelley found Woolf near the window, standing in a column of afternoon light that gave her the appearance of a person posing for a portrait that would be painted later by someone who understood that the subject was not the person but the light around the person.

"Hi," Shelley said. "I'm Shelley, from the Department."

Woolf looked at her. Woolf's way of looking at people was not the way most people do. Most people look at the surface, the face, the clothes, the posture. Woolf looked at the space around the surface, as if the person was an object in a current and the current was more interesting than the object. She looked at Shelley the way a person looks at weather, trying to determine not what it is but what it is becoming.

"You have come to improve us," Woolf said. It was not a question.

"I've come to learn about the Club," Shelley said. "To see how we might support what you're doing."

"What we are doing," Woolf repeated, "is being in a room."

"Right, but what happens in the room?"

Woolf considered this. She considered it the way she considered everything, which was slowly, thoroughly, and from an angle that made the question mean something different from what the person asking it had intended.

"The room happens in the room," she said. "We do not happen to the room. The room is not a container for activities. The room is the activity. Sitting in a room without being required to produce an outcome is the entire outcome. You cannot support that without turning it into something that requires support, and the moment it requires support, it is no longer what it was."

Shelley wrote this down. She wrote down the whole thing. I watched her pen moving, and I thought about how the act of writing down what Woolf said was itself the problem Woolf was describing. The moment the words were on paper, they became evidence. They became data. They became input for a process that would convert them into something Shelley's department could use, and the department would use them the way departments use everything, which is to extract the parts that fit the existing structure and discard the parts that do not, and what fit the structure was never the meaning, only the vocabulary.

Woolf watched the pen too. "You are translating me," she said, "into a language I did not speak."

Shelley stopped writing. For one moment, a fraction of a second, something crossed her face that was not professional warmth or active listening or departmental competence. It was the expression of a person who has heard something that she almost understands, but does not have a place to put it, and the absence of a place to put it is itself the point, but the point is uncomfortable because her training says everything should have a place.

Then the moment passed, and Shelley smiled, and the notebook opened again, and the pen resumed.

Melville intercepted Shelley at the ice station. This was not strategic. Melville did not intercept people for strategic reasons. Melville intercepted people because they had walked near the ice, and walking near the ice was an invitation to discuss the ice, the same way walking near a proud parent's desk is an invitation to discuss the photographs.

"Would you like some ice?" he asked.

"Oh, sure," Shelley said, the way people say "sure" when they believe ice is ice.

Melville poured a glass of nugget ice with the ceremonial precision of a sommelier presenting a bottle. He held the glass up to the light. The ice caught the afternoon sun and threw small scattered diamonds across the table, which Melville did not notice because he was not interested in the beauty of the ice, only in its integrity.

"This is nugget ice," he said. "It is not shaved ice. It is not cubed ice. It is not the ice that comes from the machine in the back of a gas station. This ice is from a Sonic Drive-In on Fourth Street, the one near the overpass, not the one near the mall, because the one near the mall replaced its machine in 2019, and the new machine does not understand compression. This ice," he said, placing the glass in Shelley's hand with the care of a man transferring custody of something precious, "is the correct ice."

Shelley sipped. "It's very good ice," she said, and she said it politely, generously, the way you compliment a thing that is important to someone even if you do not understand why it is important, and this was exactly the wrong thing to do because Melville did not want politeness. Melville wanted recognition. Melville wanted the kind of recognition that comes not from manners but from understanding, the recognition of a person who takes one sip and knows, truly knows, that this ice is different, that the difference matters, and that the person who brought it is not eccentric but correct.

"It is not very good ice," Melville said, gently, as a correction. "It is the good ice. There is a difference. 'Very good' is a comparison. The good ice does not compare. The good ice simply is."

Shelley wrote this down too. She was going to write everything down. She was going to take this room, this collection of people who had assembled themselves without instruction, and she was going to carry it back to the Department in a notebook, and the Department was going to look at the notebook and see what departments see, which is unstructured potential, which is the most dangerous thing a department can see because unstructured potential is the thing departments exist to structure, and structuring potential is how you kill it.

The Psychoanalyst found Shelley before she found him, because the Psychoanalyst always found people first. Finding people first was essential to his process. If you found him first, you might set the terms of the conversation, and if you set the terms of the conversation, he could not begin with his opening move, which was to observe you for three seconds and tell you something about yourself that you had not volunteered.

"You are nervous," he told Shelley.

"I'm not nervous," Shelley said.

"The portfolio," he said, nodding at the leather folder

she held against her chest like a shield. "You carry it in front of your body. Protective positioning. You feel exposed in this room because the room does not have the structure you rely on to feel competent. Without structure, you improvise, and improvisation makes you anxious because your training did not prepare you for environments that do not want your training."

Shelley stared at him.

"He does this," I said from my chair. "To everyone. It is not personal. It is a condition."

"It is observation," the Psychoanalyst said, with the wounded dignity of a man whose gift is never appreciated. "I am merely reflecting what I see."

"You are reflecting what you have decided to see," Woolf said from across the room, without turning, "and presenting the decision as if it were a mirror."

The Psychoanalyst paused. He did not often get matched, and when he did, he processed it the way a chess player processes a move he had not anticipated, not with alarm but with recalculation. He looked at Woolf. Woolf did not look back. Not looking back was Woolf's most powerful move.

"Fascinating," he said, which was his recovery word, the word he used when the conversation had gone somewhere he did not expect and he needed to reassert the appearance of being in control. "Group dynamics. The members protect each other from external assessment."

"The members," I said, "protect each other from you. That is a different thing."

Byron chose this moment to make his entrance. He had been sleeping on the windowsill for the duration of Shelley's visit, which was uncharacteristic, because Byron usually participated in any social event by making it about himself within the first four minutes. But Byron had been waiting. Whether this was instinct or calculation did not matter. The result was the same.

Byron jumped from the windowsill to the table to the back of the sofa to Shelley's tote bag in a single fluid motion that covered the entire room and knocked over a glass of water, a stack of napkins, and one of Twain's labels that had been drying on the edge of the counter.

He landed in the tote bag with the precision of a creature who has never once in his life failed to arrive exactly where he intended, and looked out from inside it with the expression of a cat who has just claimed territory and is waiting for the applause.

"Byron," Austen said.

Shelley laughed again, and this time, it was different. It was not the laugh of a person charmed by quirkiness. It was the laugh of a person who has been caught off guard by something that does not fit any of her categories, because a cat in a tote bag is not community enrichment, and it is not senior engagement, and it is not a programming opportunity. It is just a cat in a bag. It is a thing that happened, unplanned and unmanageable and pointless and alive.

"He's sweet," she said.

"He is not sweet," Austen said. "He is Byron."

Poe watched from the curtain rod. Poe had been watching Shelley since she entered. He watched her the way he watched everything, with the patient attention of a creature that does not need to understand what is happening, because understanding is a human compulsion, and he has observed over many years that the compulsion causes more problems than it solves. He watched her take notes. He watched her smile. He watched her translate the room into a language the room had not agreed to speak.

Poe shifted his weight on the curtain rod. His feathers tightened. His beak opened, just slightly, the way a beak opens when a sound is being considered but not yet authorized.

The room did not notice. The room was watching Shelley extract Byron from the tote bag, which required negotiation because Byron did not believe in extraction. Byron believed in occupation.

But I noticed. I looked up at Poe, and Poe looked down at me, and for a moment, a moment that lasted less than a second but carried the weight of something longer, the raven and I were the only two beings in the room who understood that the real assessment was not being conducted by Shelley with her notebook.

It was being conducted by the bird on the curtain rod, who had been here longer than anyone, who would be here after everyone, and who had not yet said a word.

Poe closed his beak.

Not yet.

Shelley stayed for two hours. She took eleven pages of notes. She complimented the crackers. She found three more edge pieces for the puzzle, which made Dickens so happy that he shook her hand twice and offered her a permanent seat on a subcommittee that did not exist but could be established by Wednesday if she was interested.

She asked about programming. Austen said they had none.

She asked about membership fees. Austen said there were none.

She asked about the bylaws. Austen said there were none.

She asked about goals. Austen said the Club's goal was

to continue existing, which was the same goal held by most living things and should not require paperwork.

She asked about the egg timer.

Austen reset it.

This was the complete answer.

She left at four-thirty, smiling, waving, holding her tote bag with Byron's claw marks on the interior lining. She said she would be back. She said she had ideas. She said she wanted to help.

Nobody doubted her sincerity. That was the problem. If she had been insincere, the Club could have dismissed her. If she had been hostile, the Club could have resisted her. But she was neither. She was a person who genuinely believed that what the Club had was good and that good things deserve support and support means structure and structure means documentation and documentation means that the thing you had is now the thing they have, and they will take very good care of it, and it will never be the same.

After she left, the room was quiet.

Austen stood by the pineapple.

"She will be back," he said.

"She said she would be," I said.

"She did not need to say it. She took notes. People who take notes always come back. People who take notes are building a case, even when they believe they are building a bridge." He looked at the tote bag imprint on the chair where Byron had staged his invasion. "She is not unkind," he said. "She is not incompetent. She is not dishonest."

"No," I agreed.

"She is worse than all of those things," Austen said. "She is right. She is right that we are unregistered. She is right that we have no programming. She is right that we have no documentation. She is right about everything that can be measured. And she is wrong about the only thing that matters, the reasons we work are what she is right about.

The egg timer rang.

Nobody reset it.

"She liked the ice," Melville said, into the silence, and the sentence had the weight of a man who is searching for a bright side and has found one and is holding it up for the room to see, and the room is too tired to tell him that the bright side is not bright enough.

"She used the word 'very,'" I said.

Melville nodded. His face contained the sorrow of a man who had offered someone the best thing he had and watched them receive it politely.

"There is still time," he said, and I was not sure if he meant there was still time for Shelley to understand the ice or still time for the Club to survive or still time in general, and it did not matter because the answer to all three was the same, which was yes, technically, but the clock was no longer an abstraction.

Steinbeck put his head on my shoe. Hemingway had not moved from the door. He had watched Shelley arrive and watched her leave and had not altered his position, which meant he had assessed the situation when it entered the room and saw no reason to update his assessment, and Hemingway's refusal to update an assessment was either the deepest form of confidence or the deepest form of stubbornness, and the two were, in Hemingway's case, the same thing.

Byron was cleaning himself on the table next to the pineapple, having achieved his objective for the afternoon: to insert himself into a bag, cause a minor disruption, and emerge without consequences. He had left claw marks on the inside of Shelley's tote bag, which meant that wherever Shelley went, whatever she carried in that bag, a small piece of Byron's opinion would go with her, and she would not notice it until the bag tore, and by then it would be too late.

Twain peeled the labels off the letter and applied new ones.

The top label read: **FIRST CONTACT.**

The bottom label read: **SHE'LL BE BACK.**

The bottom label was redundant. But redundancy, in Twain's philosophy, was not waste. It was emphasized. And emphasis, applied correctly, was how you made sure the record was clear even if nobody ever read it.

I went home and did not write anything. Some days, the correct response to a threat is to sit in a room with two dogs and a silence that does not require documentation. Steinbeck slept on the floor. Hemingway slept by the door.

The letter from the Department sat on my desk, next to my draft response, which was four sentences long and did not mention the pineapple and would not change anything at all. I now understood that the letter was not the beginning of the problem.

Shelley was the beginning of the problem.

And the problem with the beginning of a problem is that it always looks like help.

Chapter 3

THE BROCHURE

The brochure arrived two weeks after Shelley's visit, which was exactly the right amount of time for a department to convert eleven pages of handwritten notes into a single folded document that misunderstood everything it described. Two weeks is the bureaucratic gestation period for a certain kind of error, long enough to suggest deliberation but short enough to confirm that the deliberation was performed by people who had already decided what they were going to produce before the notes were transcribed.

It arrived in a manila envelope with the Department's tree logo in the upper left corner. The tree had not improved since the letter. It still looked like a tree designed by someone who had been told what a tree was but had never stood under one, never watched one move in the wind, never noticed that a real tree is not symmetrical and does not hold still and does not exist to represent growth on behalf of an institution. The tree on the envelope was the ghost of a tree. It was the idea of a tree after the tree had been removed.

Austen opened the envelope at the central table, next to the pineapple, with the egg timer ticking beside him. He removed the brochure the way a surgeon removes something from a patient, not with haste but with the controlled precision of a person who knows that what he is about to see may require management.

He unfolded it.

He looked at the front panel.

He said nothing.

He turned it so the room could see.

The front panel featured a photograph. The photograph showed four people who were not members of the Evergreen Club, had never been members of the Evergreen Club, and appeared to have been selected from a stock photography catalogue by someone who typed "happy seniors" into a search bar and used the first result. The four people in the photograph were smiling with the coordinated intensity of people who have been told to smile by a photographer who will not release them until the smiling reaches a threshold that the photographer alone can see. They were sitting in a sunlit room that looked like no room anyone had ever been in, a room that existed only inside the photograph and only for the duration of the shutter, a room designed to communicate warmth, togetherness, and the specific kind of joy that only exists when it is being performed for a camera.

Two of the four people were doing yoga.

Nobody in the Evergreen Club did yoga. Nobody in the Evergreen Club had expressed interest in yoga. Nobody in the Evergreen Club had, to my knowledge, ever used the word "yoga" except Woolf, who had once said, during a long silence, "Yoga is the body's attempt to apologize to itself," which was not an endorsement.

One of the remaining two people was painting. The painting was visible in the photograph. It appeared to be a sunset, or possibly a sunrise, or possibly a landscape that the painter had not yet committed to a time of day. The brush was held with the loose confidence of a person who has been given a brush by a photographer and told to look creative, and the creativity was as genuine as the smiling, which is to say it was technically present but spiritually elsewhere.

The fourth person was laughing at something off camera, which is the stock photography equivalent of being written by someone who knows a character should have emotions but does not know which ones.

Beneath the photograph, in a font that managed to be simultaneously cheerful and institutional, were the words:

THE EVERGREEN CLUB Where Community Comes Alive!

"Alive," Twain said. She said it once, the way a person says a word they intend to dismantle. She reached for the label maker. The label was already forming in her mind before her hand touched the machine. I could see it in her face, the way you can see a sneeze before it arrives.

"Wait," Austen said.

"I cannot wait," Twain said. "The word 'alive' has been used as if it is a selling point. We are already alive. Alive is the minimum. Alive is not an accomplishment for a club. It is an accomplishment for a patient."

"Wait until we have read the full document."

"I can label and listen simultaneously. Labeling is not an obstacle to listening. Labeling is how I listen. If I do not label, the words have no place to go, and they pile up, and the pile becomes unmanageable, and that is how organizations lose control of their vocabulary."

Austen did not argue. Arguing with Twain about labeling was structurally identical to arguing with Melville about ice: the argument itself became evidence for the other person's position, because if labeling were not important, then why would you spend so much energy resisting it, and if it were not necessary, then why did the absence of it cause such visible distress?

Austen opened the brochure to the inside panels.

The left panel was headed **OUR MISSION**. This was the first time the Evergreen Club had been assigned a mission, and the mission was assigned the way weather is assigned in a forecast, by people who were not present for the actual conditions but had access to instruments they trusted more than observation.

The mission read:

"The Evergreen Club is a vibrant community space dedicated to fostering connection, wellness, and lifelong enrichment among older adults in a supportive and inclusive environment. Through structured programming, creative engagement, and intergenerational dialogue, the Evergreen Club empowers its members to live with purpose, vitality, and joy."

Austen read this aloud. He read it the way a man reads a verdict, evenly, without emphasis, allowing the words to convict themselves. When he finished, the room was quiet for a period that the egg timer would have measured as approximately four seconds but that felt longer because four seconds of silence after the word "joy" is used to describe a room that contains a raven, an unexplained pineapple, and a man who guards fast food ice with paramilitary devotion is a particular kind of four seconds.

"Vibrant," Twain said. She printed the first label. It read: **VIBRANT** (1).

"Connection," Dickens said, brightening, because Dickens heard the word "connection" the way some people hear a starting gun. "Well, that is not entirely wrong. We do connect. We are connecting right now. I am connected to this puzzle. Melville is connected to his ice. Twain is connected to her labels. We are a network of connections. If they want to call that a mission, I can see the logic. I can see the structure. I can build on this. I can have a flowchart by Tuesday."

"Dickens," Austen said.

"A small flowchart."

"No."

Dickens deflated, but only temporarily, the way a balloon deflates when it is not punctured but merely released at the opening and can be reinflated with the next breath, and Dickens always had a next breath.

Woolf had taken the brochure from Austen's hands without asking, the way Woolf took things, not with force but with the quiet certainty of a person who believes that objects gravitate toward whoever needs them most, and Woolf always needed documents most because Woolf read them differently from everyone else. She did not read for content. She read for weight. She read the way a person listens to music, attending not to the notes but to the spaces between them, and the spaces in this brochure were enormous.

"Empowers," she said, holding the word at arm's length as if it were damp. "They have used the word 'empowers.' As if power is a thing that can be given by a brochure. As if we are sitting here in a state of diminished power, and the Department, through the mechanism of structured programming, will restore what time has taken. The word assumes we have been disempowered. The word assumes the solution is external. The word is a door that opens only from the outside."

She set the brochure down on the table next to the pineapple. The pineapple and the brochure sat side by side, and the contrast was the contrast between a thing that had never explained itself and a thing that could not stop explaining itself, and the brochure looked worse for the comparison, the way all explanations look worse next to the thing they are trying to explain.

The center panel of the brochure was headed PROGRAMMING, and beneath that heading was a list. The list was the most dangerous part of the brochure because lists imply sequence and sequence implies planning and planning implies management and management implies that the thing being managed cannot manage itself, and the entire history of the Evergreen Club was a demonstration that it could manage itself perfectly well as long as nobody tried to help.

The programming list read:

Monday: Wellness Hour (chair yoga, guided meditation, health discussions) Wednesday: Creative Expression (art, writing, music appreciation) Friday: Community Dialogue (current events, storytelling, intergenerational panels)

"Chair yoga," I said.

"Chair yoga," Austen confirmed.

"We are being offered chair yoga."

"We are being offered chair yoga, guided meditation, and health discussions on Mondays. Creative expression on Wednesdays. Community dialogue on Fridays. The brochure assumes we are available on Mondays, Wednesdays, and Fridays. The brochure assumes we want to express ourselves creatively on a schedule. The brochure assumes we are in need of dialogue with the community and that the community is in need of dialogue with us, and that this dialogue requires a panel."

"An intergenerational panel," I said.

"An intergenerational panel," Austen repeated, and the word "intergenerational" settled over the room like a weather system. It was a word that meant, in practice, that younger people would be brought in to sit across from older people and ask them questions about what it was like to be older, and the older people would answer, and the answers would be treated as quaint and valuable and ultimately decorative, the way a museum treats the objects it displays, with respect and care and the unspoken understanding that the objects are no longer in use.

The Psychoanalyst was reading the brochure over Woolf's shoulder, which Woolf permitted the way a country permits a neighboring nation to observe its borders, with awareness, tolerance, and the understanding that one wrong step would trigger a proportional response.

"This is actually quite thoughtful," the Psychoanalyst said.

The room looked at him.

"The programming addresses multiple domains. Physical wellness. Creative outlet. Social engagement. It is a holistic approach to the aging experience."

"It is a holistic approach to the appearance of addressing the aging experience," I said. "The aging experience does not require a panel. The aging experience requires a chair that does not have the word 'yoga' in front of it."

"There you go again," the Psychoanalyst said, with the fond exasperation of a teacher whose favorite student keeps making the same instructive mistake. "Resistance to support. It is very common among people who have built their identity around self-sufficiency. The offer of help is experienced as an accusation of helplessness."

"The offer of help," I said, "is experienced as an offer of help that we did not request from people who have not been in this room long enough to know that the egg timer rings and nobody asks why."

"And why does nobody ask why?"

"Because asking why the egg timer rings is the same as asking why the pineapple is here, and asking why the pineapple is here is the first step toward explaining the pineapple, and explaining the pineapple is the first step toward losing the pineapple."

The Psychoanalyst nodded slowly. "So the pineapple is a defense mechanism."

"The pineapple is a pineapple."

"Nothing is just a pineapple."

"This pineapple is."

He smiled the smile of a man who has been told the sky is not blue and considers the denial more interesting than the color. He was making a note in the small leather journal he carried, which was different from Shelley's notebook in that Shelley's notebook was institutional, and the Psychoanalyst's journal was personal, which made it worse because personal notes become convictions and convictions become interventions and interventions become the Psychoanalyst sitting in your most comfortable chair telling you that your fruit is a metaphor.

Melville had been studying the brochure from a distance, the way a person studies a thing they are not sure they want to touch. He had been quiet, which was unusual for Melville during a crisis, but the brochure had not mentioned ice, and the omission had placed him in a particular kind of shock, the shock of a person whose primary concern had been so thoroughly ignored that he was not sure whether to be offended or relieved.

"There is nothing about ice," he said.

"There is nothing about ice," Austen confirmed.

"They have listed wellness. They have listed creative expression. They have listed community dialogue. They have not listed ice. They have not even listed refreshments. They have listed chair yoga, which requires a chair, and they have listed guided meditation, which requires a guide, and they have listed health discussions, which require health, but they have not listed ice, which requires only ice, and the correct ice at that, and the absence of the correct ice in a document that claims to be about wellness is a contradiction so fundamental that I do not know how to respond to it except to say that any organization that believes wellness can be achieved without the correct ice has misunderstood wellness at a level that cannot be repaired by programming."

This was, by Melville's standards, a short speech. He had once delivered a forty-minute address on the difference between nugget ice and pellet ice to a room that had not asked. The restraint he was showing now was the restraint of a man who has been so deeply wounded that eloquence has replaced volume, the way a very angry person sometimes becomes very quiet and the quiet is louder than the shouting would have been.

Byron jumped onto the table, circled the brochure twice with the investigative focus of a creature cataloguing a new object in his territory, and sat on it. This was Byron's review. Byron's reviews were always physical. He did not critique with nuance. He critiqued with his entire body. The brochure was now partially obscured by a young cat who had decided it was a surface, and surfaces, in Byron's world, existed to be occupied, and occupation was the only opinion that mattered.

"Get off the brochure," Austen said, without conviction.

Byron looked at Austen with the expression of a cat who has heard a request, is weighing it against his own preferences, and has found it lacking.

He did not move.

"Leave him," I said. "He is the most honest critic in the room."

The right panel of the brochure, which Austen recovered by gently sliding it from beneath Byron, who permitted this with the tolerant disdain of a creature who considers all human actions beneath him but allows them to continue because the alternative is effort, contained the section that Austen had been saving.

It was headed **OUR SYMBOL**.

Beneath the heading was a small illustration of a pineapple. It was not a photograph of our pineapple. It was a graphic, a clip art rendering of a pineapple that looked the way all clip art looks; it looked like the memory of a thing rather than the thing itself. It was a pineapple that had been processed through a design program and emerged on the other side, smoother, simpler, and entirely without the particular quality that made our pineapple ours: its weight, its presence, its refusal to explain or accommodate or be anything other than exactly what it was.

Beneath the clip art pineapple were the words:

"The pineapple is a traditional symbol of welcome and hospitality. At the Evergreen Club, our pineapple represents our commitment to creating a warm, inclusive space where every member feels valued and at home."

Austen read this aloud.

Then he read it again.

He read it the second time the way a person reads a sentence that has personally wronged them, slowly, with the kind of attention that is usually reserved for contracts and threats. Each word received its own moment. "Traditional." Pause. "Symbol." Pause. "Welcome." Pause. And then the word that landed in the room like a stone dropped into still water: "Hospitality."

"Hospitality," Austen said.

The pineapple sat on the table. The real pineapple. The actual pineapple that had sat in that spot since the Club's founding, and had never once welcomed anyone, never once been hospitable, and never once represented a commitment to warmth or inclusion or the feeling of being valued. The pineapple did not welcome. The pineapple presided. The pineapple existed in the center of the room the way a monument exists in the center of a square, not because it is inviting but because it was placed there by someone whose reasons have been forgotten and whose authority has been replaced by the authority of the object itself, which is the authority of things that have been in a place long enough that removing them would be more disruptive than leaving them and explaining them would be more dangerous than silence.

"They have explained the pineapple," Austen said.

He said it the way a general says, "They have crossed the border." Not with panic. Not with surprise. With the flat recognition of a man who knew this was coming and prepared for it and is now confronting the difference between preparing for a thing and experiencing the thing, which is the same difference as the difference between knowing you will get old and being old, the preparation is useful but insufficient, and the experience is not what the preparation described.

"They have explained the pineapple and the explanation is wrong, and the wrongness does not matter because the explanation is now in print and print is permanent and permanent is policy and policy is the thing we were told to prevent."

He looked at me.

I looked at the brochure. Byron was sitting on the corner of it again. The clip art pineapple was visible beneath his tail, which was an editorial comment that I did not need to interpret because it interpreted itself.

"I told you," I said, "that the letter would not change anything."

"You did."

"I told you that four sentences would not be enough."

"You did. And you were correct. And the correctness does not help because being correct about a problem is not the same as solving a problem, and you are a writer, and writers are often correct about problems and almost never the ones who solve them, because solving problems requires a different kind of sentence than the kind you write, and the kind of sentence that solves problems is the kind of sentence that appears in bylaws and memoranda and organizational charts, and those sentences are Dickens's department, and Dickens's department produces sentences that multiply faster than the problems they describe."

Dickens looked up from the puzzle. He had been quietly working during the brochure reading, which was his way of processing the crisis, the way Melville's was ice, Twain's was labels, and Woolf's was staring into a light source until the light source became a metaphor. Dickens processed crisis through productivity. If the world were falling apart, Dickens would build a shelf. If the shelf was falling apart, Dickens would build a shelf for the shelf. The shelves would not save anyone, but they would be well constructed, and Dickens would feel that construction was itself a form of resistance, and he was not entirely wrong.

"I can draft a counterbrochure," Dickens said. "A better brochure. A brochure that describes what we actually are. I can have it done by the weekend. It will be thorough. It will be comprehensive. It will have sections, subsections, a table of contents, an appendix, and a fold-out map of the room with the seating arrangement annotated."

"A fold out map," Austen said.

"It adds dimensionality."

"We do not need dimensionality. We need the Department to stop explaining our pineapple."

"The counterbrochure could address the pineapple directly. We could include a section titled 'Regarding the Pineapple' and leave it blank. Just the heading and blank space. That would make the point."

Everyone in the room considered this. It was, by Dickens's standards, an elegant idea, possibly the most elegant idea Dickens had ever produced. A blank section headed "Regarding the Pineapple" would say everything by saying nothing, which was exactly what the pineapple itself did, and reproducing the pineapple's method in print was a kind of tribute that the pineapple probably would not appreciate because the pineapple did not appreciate things, but the rest of us could appreciate it on the pineapple's behalf.

"No counterbrochure," Austen said. "A counterbrochure is a response, and a response is an engagement, and an engagement is a relationship, and a relationship with a department is a relationship you do not end. You manage it. And we are not in the business of managing relationships with departments. We are in the business of sitting in a room with a pineapple."

Twain had been labeling steadily throughout the discussion. She had labeled the brochure itself with three separate labels. The first read: UNSOLICITED. The second read: INACCURATE. The third, applied directly over the clip art pineapple, read: THIS IS NOT OUR PINEAPPLE.

She held up the brochure for the room to see. The labels covered approximately forty percent of the front panel. This was, for Twain, a proportional response. The brochure was forty percent wrong. Forty percent of the brochure was now corrected. Mathematics supported her position. She was satisfied.

"I have an additional label," she said, "that I would like to apply to the section about our mission, but I need a ruling from Austen because the label contains language that some members may find direct."

"What does the label say?" Austen asked.

"FICTION."

"Apply it," Austen said.

Twain applied it. The label read FICTION in capital letters across the mission statement, and the mission statement looked better for it, the way a building looks better when someone posts a condemnation notice on the door because at least the condemnation notice is honest about what the building is.

Poe shifted on the curtain rod.

The movement was small. A rearrangement of weight. A tightening of feathers along the shoulders that made the raven look slightly larger, slightly more present, the way a person looks when they sit forward in a meeting because something has been said that they have been waiting for someone to say.

Poe opened his beak.

The room did not stop. The room did not notice. The

room was still processing the brochure, still labeling, still debating, still being the room it always was, which was a room where every person believed their particular expertise was the one that would solve the current problem, and every person was wrong in a way that was entirely consistent with their character.

But I noticed. I was in my chair, the chair that had been through things, and I was watching the raven the way you watch a person who is about to speak for the first time in a conversation that has been going on for years. Poe's beak was open. The angle was deliberate. The throat moved, a small muscular contraction that precedes vocalization in birds, the mechanical preparation for a sound that the bird has decided to make but has not yet released.

The sound did not come.

Poe's beak closed. Slowly. With the precise control of a creature that has chosen silence not because it has nothing to say but because what it has to say is not yet ready to be heard, or the room is not yet ready to hear it, or the timing is not yet correct, and Poe, unlike every other being in this room, had the patience to wait for correct timing because correct timing was not a human skill. Correct timing was a bird's skill. And birds, unlike humans, do not speak because they are expected to. Birds speak because it is time.

I looked at Poe. Poe looked at me. The same look as before. The same understanding. The raven knew something that the rest of the room would learn later, and the raven was content to let them learn it on their own schedule.

Hemingway was still by the door. He had not moved during the reading of the brochure. He had assessed the brochure the way he assessed everything: to determine whether it required his attention, determine that it did not, and remain in his position, because Hemingway's position was his statement, and his statement was his position, and the two were the same thing and neither required elaboration.

Steinbeck was asleep. Steinbeck's ability to sleep during a crisis was not indifference. It was trust. Steinbeck trusted the room to handle its own problems the way he trusted the floor to hold his weight. The floor had never failed him. The room had never failed him. Steinbeck was the only member of the Club who did not worry about the future, not because he lacked the capacity but because he had decided, at some fundamental level of his being, that the people around him would manage, and if they did not manage, he would still be here, and being here was enough.

Byron was still on the brochure. He had fallen asleep in the exact position of a cat who has defeated something and is resting on its corpse.

The egg timer rang.

Austen reset it.

The interval began.

"What do we do?" Dickens asked, and the question was the question of a man who has a toolbox and is looking for the nail, any nail, the correct nail being a secondary concern when the primary concern is the use of the tool.

"We wait," Austen said.

"For what?"

"For the next thing. The brochure is the second step. There will be a third step. The third step will be more concrete. It will involve a meeting. The meeting will involve a proposal. The proposal will involve money. And when it involves money, the conversation will change, because money is the thing that turns an idea into an institution, and an institution is the thing that turns a room into a program, and a program is the thing that turns us into clients."

He touched the pineapple, briefly, the way a person touches a wall to confirm it is still solid.

"We wait," he said again. "And we do what we do, which is nothing, and nothing is what we do best, and nothing is the thing they cannot put in a brochure."

I took the brochure home. I placed it on my desk next to the four-sentence letter that had not changed anything. Hemingway looked at both documents from across the room, unimpressed by the letter, unimpressed by the brochure, unimpressed by the desk, unimpressed by the situation, and entirely sure that his position by the door was the correct response to all of it.

Steinbeck slept on the floor, trusting.

I looked at the clip art pineapple on the brochure and thought about the real pineapple on the table and the distance between them, which was not a distance measured in miles or inches but in the difference between a thing that is alive and a thing that is a picture of a thing that is alive, and the difference is everything, and the brochure did not know it, and Shelley did not know it, and the Department did not know it, and the only ones who knew it were the people in the room and the raven on the curtain rod and the pineapple itself, which knew it the way all real things know that they are real, which is by not needing to be told.

Private Ledger Entry:

They explained the pineapple. On paper. In clip art. I keep thinking about the dent it doesn't have yet. The one it will get if this keeps going. My hand hurts from writing the four sentence letter that did nothing. Dogs don't care. They just want the floor and the door. I want the floor, the door, and the pineapple that stays unexplained.

Chapter 4

THE GRANT

The grant arrived the way all money arrives when you have not asked for it: with conditions attached and a smile that implies you should be grateful.

Shelley presented it at the third meeting she attended, which was the meeting where she stopped asking questions and started answering them, which is the moment any visitor becomes an occupant, and occupants have opinions about the furniture. She had moved from observation to implementation without announcing the transition, the way a river moves from flowing alongside a field to flowing through it, and by the time you notice the difference, the field is already wet, and the river considers the new path established.

She placed the grant application on the table next to the pineapple. The document was thirty-two pages long, printed on one side, bound with a clear plastic cover and a blue backing that gave it the appearance of a high school report that had been promoted beyond its qualifications. The cover page read:

COMMUNITY ENRICHMENT PARTNERSHIP GRANT Department of Community Enrichment and Senior Engagement Application for Organizational Development Funding Fiscal Year 2025-2026

Beneath the title was the tree logo, still unconvincing, still committed to the idea that it was a tree despite all visual evidence to the contrary. The tree had been joined by a small sun in the upper right corner, suggesting that the Department's design team had been given a budget increase or a second clip art subscription and, in either case, had used the new resources to add celestial bodies to a logo that did not need them.

"I have wonderful news," Shelley said.

Shelley always had wonderful news. Wonderful news was her primary export. She arrived at every meeting carrying wonderful news the way Melville arrived carrying ice, with the absolute conviction that the thing she was bringing was the thing the room needed, and the room's failure to request it was an oversight that her presence corrected.

"The Department has identified funding," she said. "The Community Enrichment Partnership Grant provides up to forty-eight thousand dollars over two years for qualifying community organizations. I've reviewed the criteria. The Evergreen Club qualifies."

She said "qualifies" with the satisfied brightness of a person delivering a medical result that came back negative, as if qualifying for a grant was the same as passing a test, and passing a test meant the patient was healthy, and the patient in this case was the Club, and the Club had been diagnosed as eligible for treatment it had not sought.

"Forty-eight thousand dollars," Dickens said.

He said it with the reverence of a man who has just

been told that a new wing of the building has been approved and all he needs to do is design it. Forty-eight thousand dollars was, to Dickens, not money. It was surface area. It was whiteboards, subcommittees, flowcharts, and organizational structures that could finally be built with the weight of funding behind them. Forty-eight thousand dollars was the difference between a plan that existed on a napkin and a plan that existed in the world, and Dickens had napkins full of plans that had been waiting their entire lives for exactly this moment.

"Over two years," Shelley clarified. "Twenty-four thousand per year. It covers a part-time coordinator, programming materials, facility improvements, and administrative costs."

"A part-time coordinator," Austen said.

He said it the way a homeowner says "termites." Not with alarm. With the flat recognition that something has entered the structure, the structure will need to be assessed.

"Yes," Shelley said. "Someone to manage scheduling, communications, and member engagement. The coordinator would report to the board of directors."

"We do not have a board of directors," Austen said.

"The grant requires one."

"Then the grant requires something we do not have and did not seek."

"That's actually one of the things the grant helps you establish. The first phase is organizational development. Bylaws, board formation, mission statement, and strategic plan. The funding supports the process of becoming a formal organization."

"We are not a formal organization."

"Right, and this helps you become one."

"We do not wish to become one."

Shelley paused. This was the pause of a person who had encountered a response that her training did not predict, the way a GPS pauses when you drive off the mapped road. The GPS does not panic. The GPS recalculates. Shelley was recalculating.

"I understand there might be some hesitation," she said. "Change can feel uncomfortable. But the funding would allow you to do so much more than what you're doing now."

The sentence landed in the room, and the room received it the way a courtroom receives a statement that the witness does not realize is a confession. "So much more than what you're doing now." The sentence assumed that what the Club was doing now was insufficient. The sentence assumed that more was better. The sentence assumed that the Club wanted to do more and was being prevented by a lack of funding, the way a car wants to go faster and is being prevented by a lack of fuel, and all Shelley was offering was fuel, and the car should be grateful.

But the Club was not a car. The Club was a room with a pineapple in it. And the room with the pineapple in it did not want to go faster. The room with the pineapple was not going anywhere. That was the point. The entire architectural principle of the Evergreen Club was that it existed without velocity, without trajectory, without a destination that could be measured or a progress that could be reported. The Club was not on its way to becoming something. The Club was the thing it was, and the thing it was did not require forty-eight thousand dollars to continue being.

But money is a particular kind of argument, and the particular thing about money as an argument is that it does not need to be right. It only needs to be present. The presence of money changes the weight of every other argument in the room, the way the presence of a large planet changes the orbits of smaller objects around it. You do not need to agree with the money. You only need to be near it, and being near it bends your path, and the bending is so gradual that you do not notice you have changed direction until you are somewhere you did not intend to be.

I could feel the room bending.

Dickens was already reading the application. He had turned to the section on organizational structure and was studying it with the focused delight of a man who has found a blueprint for a building he has been designing in his head for years. "This is quite thorough," he said. "Board composition. Committee structure. Reporting timelines. Annual reviews. There is even a section on succession planning."

"Succession planning," I said.

"For leadership transitions. In case Austen is unable to continue as host."

Austen looked at Dickens with the expression of a man who had just been told that his house had been appraised by someone who had not been invited inside. "I am the host," Austen said. "I do not require a succession plan. A succession plan implies the host is a position. The host is not a position. The host is me. I am not a position that another person will fill. I am a person who opens the door, resets the egg timer, and makes sure the furniture is trained and the pineapple is undisturbed. These are not transferable skills. These are personal qualities that happen to manifest as hosting."

"But what if something happens to you," Dickens said,

with the innocent pragmatism of a man who does not realize he has just asked someone to contemplate their own replacement.

"If something happens to me," Austen said, "the door will remain open, the timer will continue to ring, and the pineapple will continue to preside, because none of these things depend on me. They depend on the room. And the room does not need a succession plan. The room needs to be left alone."

Shelley was taking notes. She was always taking notes. The notes were the most dangerous thing in the room because the notes would survive the conversation and the conversation would not, and when the conversation was over, and the notes were reviewed in an office with fluorescent lighting and a tree logo, the notes would say whatever the notes said, and the conversation would not be there to object.

"Can I walk you through the key requirements?" Shelley asked, and she asked it the way a tour guide asks if you would like to see the next room, as if the tour is optional and you are free to decline, but the tour guide is already walking, and declining means standing alone in the hallway.

"Please," Austen said, because Austen was a host, and a host does not refuse information even when the information is a siege.

Shelley opened the application to a tabbed section labeled GOVERNANCE REQUIREMENTS.

"The grant requires a board of directors with a minimum of five members," she said. "The board must include at least one member under the age of forty to represent intergenerational engagement."

"Under forty," Twain said. "In a club where the average age is older than most of the furniture."

"It's a diversity requirement. The Department believes that intergenerational representation strengthens organizational governance."

"The Department," Twain said, "believes that putting a young person on a board of older people is a form of representation. What it actually is, is a form of decoration. The young person is not there to govern. The young person is there to be pointed at during inspections. 'Look,' the Department says, 'they have a young person. They are intergenerational. Give them the money.' The young person is a garnish. A regulatory garnish. And I say this as a person who appreciates labels, and who understands that every label is, at some level, a fiction agreed upon by the people who apply it and the people who read it, but this particular fiction is more fictional than most."

She printed a label. It read: **GARNISH REQUIREMENT.**

Shelley continued, undeterred, because Shelley had the professional resilience of a person whose job required her to walk into rooms full of people who did not want what she was offering and offer it anyway, and the offering was her purpose, and the purpose sustained her the way Melville was sustained by ice, with the simple faith that the thing she carried was the right thing and the room would come to understand this if she stayed long enough and smiled consistently enough and took enough notes.

"The grant also requires quarterly reports," she said. "Attendance records, activity logs, member satisfaction surveys, and a narrative progress report submitted to the Department by the fifteenth of each quarter."

"Quarterly reports," Austen said.

"To demonstrate outcomes."

"What outcomes?"

"Member engagement. Wellness metrics. Programming participation. Community impact."

"The outcome of the Evergreen Club," Austen said, "is that it exists. That is the outcome. It exists, people come to it, and while they are here, they are not being measured, surveyed, reported on, or asked to demonstrate impact. They are sitting in a room. They are being in a room. The outcome is the room. The room is the outcome. And you cannot put a room in a quarterly report because the room is not a metric. The room is a room."

"I understand," Shelley said, and she said "I understand" the way people say "I understand" when they do not understand but have been trained to say it because saying "I understand" creates the appearance of listening and the appearance of listening creates the conditions for continuing to talk, and continuing to talk was Shelley's primary strategy because Shelley believed that if she explained the grant clearly enough, the clarity would convert the reluctance, and she did not yet understand that the reluctance was not caused by a lack of clarity but by an excess of it. The Club understood the grant perfectly. That was the problem.

Melville had been quiet. Melville had been quiet for longer than Melville was usually quiet, which was itself a kind of statement, because Melville's silence was always the silence of a man who is thinking about ice and waiting for the conversation to arrive at the point where ice becomes relevant. And now it had.

"The grant," Melville said. "Does it cover equipment?"

"Equipment is an eligible expense under facility improvements," Shelley said.

"Kitchen equipment?"

"If it serves the organization's programming needs, yes."

Melville set down his bag of nugget ice. He set it down the way a man sets down a weapon, not because he has surrendered but because he no longer needs it. He set it down with the care of a person who loves a thing and is placing it gently aside because something larger has appeared on the horizon, something he has wanted for so long that wanting it has become a permanent feature of his personality, like a limp or an accent, and now the wanting might end, and the ending of the wanting is more disorienting than the wanting itself.

"An ice machine," Melville said.

He said it the way a man in a desert says "water." He said it the way a pilgrim says the name of the destination after years of walking. He said it with the quiet intensity of a person who has carried a single conviction through every room he has ever entered and is now standing in a room where the conviction might become real.

"A proper ice machine. A nugget ice machine. Commercial grade. The Scotsman SCN60. It produces sixty pounds of nugget ice per day. It has a fifteen-pound storage capacity. It fits under a standard counter. It understands compression."

He looked at Shelley. "Does the grant cover a Scotsman SCN60?"

"If it's included in the budget proposal as a facility improvement, I don't see why not."

Melville sat down. He sat down the way a man sits down when something inside him has shifted, the way furniture shifts in a house that has settled. The bag of ice was still on the table. The bag of ice was still the good ice, from the Sonic Drive-In on Fourth Street near the overpass, not the one near the mall. But the bag of ice was now sitting next to a future in which the bag of ice would not be necessary, because the machine would produce the ice and the machine would produce it here, in this room, on demand, forever, and the bag would be retired with full honors, and Melville could stop making the drive and stop worrying about condensation and stop defending his choice to people who did not understand it, because the machine would validate what the bag had only promised.

"Melville," Austen said.

Melville looked up. His face was the face of a man caught between two loyalties, which is the face all faces eventually become if you live long enough to accumulate loyalties that conflict.

"The ice machine would be very good," Melville said.

"The ice machine would be the grant's ice machine," Austen said. "It would be purchased with the grant's money. It would be reported in the grant's quarterly filings. It would be inventoried as the grant's equipment. If the grant ends, the ice machine's ownership becomes a matter of departmental policy. The ice machine would belong to them."

Melville looked at his bag. He looked at the grant application. He looked at the bag again.

"They would own the ice," he said.

"They would own the machine that makes the ice. Whether they would own the ice itself is a legal question I am not prepared to answer, but the machine would be theirs, and a man whose ice comes from another man's machine is a man whose ice can be taken away, and ice that can be taken away is not the good ice. The good ice is the ice you carry yourself."

Melville picked up the bag. He held it the way a man holds a thing he almost traded for something easier and is now holding tighter because the almost trading revealed the value that familiarity had hidden.

"The bag stays," Melville said.

"The bag stays," Austen agreed.

But the room had cracked. Not broken. Cracked. The crack was the width of a Scotsman SCN60, and the crack was real, and everyone in the room had seen it, and the crack was the thing that money does to rooms that have been operating on principle. Principle is strong. Principle is durable. Principle has held this room together since its founding. But principle does not produce sixty pounds of nugget ice per day, and the gap between principle and ice is the gap through which institutions enter.

The Psychoanalyst had been watching the exchange between Austen and Melville with the rapt attention of a person at a tennis match who believes both players are actually playing a different game than the one the audience sees.

"This is very rich," he said.

"Please don't," I said.

"The ice machine is not about ice. The ice machine is about legitimacy. Melville has been carrying ice from an external source because the Club has never been able to provide what he needs internally. The grant offers internal provision. The resistance to the grant is the resistance to being provided for, because being provided for means acknowledging a need, and acknowledging a need means accepting dependence, and accepting dependence means the self-sufficient identity of the Club is a story the Club tells itself rather than a condition the Club actually maintains."

"The ice machine," Melville said, with the gravity of a man correcting a fundamental misapprehension, "is about ice."

"Nothing is about what it appears to be about."

"Ice is."

"You believe that because the alternative is threatening."

"I believe that because I have carried ice to this room every week for three years and I know what ice is and I know what ice is about and ice is about ice and you are about something else entirely and the something else is the reason nobody in this room asks you for your opinion and you give it anyway."

This was the longest thing Melville had ever said that was not about ice, except that it was about ice, because everything Melville said was about ice even when it appeared to be about something else, which was exactly the opposite of what the Psychoanalyst believed, which was that everything anyone said was about something else even when it appeared to be about the thing, and the two positions were irreconcilable and had been irreconcilable since the first day both men entered the same room and would remain irreconcilable until one of them left, and neither of them was leaving, which meant the irreconciliation was permanent and the room had absorbed it the way the room absorbed everything, which was by continuing to exist around it.

Steinbeck, sensing the elevated emotion, put his head on Melville's foot. Steinbeck did not take sides. Steinbeck provided comfort the way the floor provided support, unconditionally, structurally, and without any expectation of recognition. Melville looked down at the dog. The dog looked up at Melville. Something passed between them that was not therapeutic and not analytical and not institutional and not subject to quarterly reporting. It was just a man and a dog and a bag of ice and the quiet agreement that some things are exactly what they are.

Hemingway remained by the door. Hemingway had assessed the grant application when it entered the room and had not altered his assessment. The grant application was a thing that had come through the door, and things that came through the door were either threats or not threats, and this one was a threat, and Hemingway's response to threats was to position himself between the threat and the room and wait, because waiting was a strategy and the door was a position and the combination of the two was the most Hemingway could offer and it was, in its way, enough.

Byron had climbed onto Shelley's portfolio and was kneading it with the focused aggression of a cat who has found expensive leather and intends to express himself on it. The portfolio was developing small puncture marks. Shelley did not notice. She was reviewing the timeline section of the grant application with Dickens, who had produced a napkin and was already sketching a project plan that included milestones, deliverables, and a Gantt chart that he was drawing freehand with a confidence that suggested he believed Henry Gantt had personally endorsed this method.

Twain had labeled the grant application. The front cover now bore four labels. CONDITIONAL. INSTITU-TIONAL. EXTERNAL AUTHORITY. And, in smaller print along the bottom edge, TROJAN.

She had also labeled Shelley's pen, which Shelley had

left on the table during the ice machine discussion. The pen now read: INSTRUMENT OF RECORD.

Woolf had not spoken since the grant was introduced. She was standing by the open window, and the air coming through it was moving the curtain in a pattern that Woolf watched, the way a person watches a fire, not for warmth but for the way the movement makes time visible. The curtain moved. The air moved. Woolf moved with them in the way she moved with everything, slightly behind, slightly to the side, occupying the space between what was happening and what it meant.

"It is not the money," she said, finally, speaking to the window or to the air or to the curtain or to all three. "The money is a translation. The money says: we will give you resources in exchange for your language. Speak our language. File our reports. Use our words. Call yourselves what we call you. And in exchange, you will have a machine that makes ice, a coordinator who manages your schedule, and a board that governs your future. The exchange is not equal. It is never equal. The money is always more than it appears, and the cost is always more than it states. The money is a door that opens from the outside, and once it is open, you cannot close it from the inside because the hinges are theirs."

She turned from the window.

"I have opened doors like that before," she said. "They do not close when you want them to. They close when the money decides."

The room was quiet.

The egg timer rang.

Austen reset it. He reset it with the careful, deliberate motion of a man performing a ritual that has become, in this moment, more important than it has ever been, because the ritual is the thing the grant cannot buy, the report cannot measure, and the brochure cannot describe. The timer rings. The timer is reset. No one asks why. Everyone nods. The interval begins. This is the Club. This is what the Club does. This is what forty-eight thousand dollars cannot purchase because it is not for sale, and the things that are not for sale are the things that institutions most want to own because the not-for-sale quality is the quality that makes them work, and owning the quality destroys it, and the destruction is permanent, and the institution will never understand why the thing stopped working after they bought it.

"We will discuss this further next week," Austen said.

"The application deadline is the thirtieth," Shelley said.

"Then we will discuss it before the thirtieth."

"It would be helpful to have a preliminary consensus before I start the budget section."

"There is no preliminary consensus. There is a pineapple and an egg timer and a room full of people who have not yet decided whether forty-eight thousand dollars is worth the price of forty-eight thousand dollars, a question that sounds absurd until you understand that the price of money is never the money. The price of money is what you agree to in order to receive it."

Shelley nodded. She nodded the way a person nods when they believe the conversation will continue and the continuation will produce the result they expect, because Shelley still believed that the result was inevitable, that the money would be accepted because money is always accepted because money is the argument that does not need to be right, and she was not wrong about that, she was not wrong about any of it, and her rightness was the problem, and the problem was getting closer, and the egg timer was ticking, and the pineapple was not helping.

I walked home with Steinbeck and Hemingway. Steinbeck walked the way Steinbeck always walked, with the steady, uncomplicated gait of a creature who trusts the ground. Hemingway walked ahead, checking corners, assessing the route, maintaining the perimeter he had established around our lives the first day he arrived and had never relaxed, because relaxing a perimeter was the same as abandoning it, and Hemingway did not abandon positions.

At home, I sat at the desk. The brochure was still there. The four-sentence letter was still there. And now the grant application existed somewhere in the world, thirty-two pages of conditions and requirements and quarterly reports and board compositions, all of it reasonable, all of it professional, all of it aimed at a room that did not want to be aimed at by anything.

Hemingway sat by the door. Steinbeck sat at my feet. Neither of them had an opinion about the grant. Neither of them required forty-eight thousand dollars to continue being what they were. Neither of them had ever been offered a Scotsman SCN60 and felt the pull of a loyalty they did not know they could be tempted to betray.

The bag of ice was still at the Club, on the table, next to the pineapple, where Melville had left it. Tomorrow it would be water. The day after that, Melville would bring a new bag from the Sonic Drive-In on Fourth Street, the one near the overpass, because the bag was always temporary and the commitment was always permanent, and the difference between those two things was the difference between a grant and a room, and the room would still be here when the grant was spent.

I hoped.

. . .

PRIVATE LEDGER ENTRY:

Melville almost traded the bag for a machine. I almost traded the room for four sentences that worked. The grant is forty-eight thousand dollars of other people's certainty. My certainty fits in one chair, two dogs, and whatever is left of the person who still shows up. The timer rang while I was thinking this. I nodded anyway.

Chapter 5

THE SURVEY

The surveys arrived in a box. Not an envelope, not a folder, not a polite stack held together with a paper clip and a prayer. A box. A cardboard box with the Department's tree logo stamped on the side, the tree still failing to convince anyone that it had ever been a tree, and beside the tree a new addition: the word SURVEY printed in a font that managed to be both friendly and compulsory, the typographical equivalent of a person who smiles while handing you a subpoena.

Shelley carried the box with the careful pride of a person delivering something she had worked on, something she believed would be useful, something she had designed with the genuine intention of understanding the Club's needs so that she could better serve those needs, and the genuineness was the thing that made the box so heavy, because a box full of cynical surveys could be dismissed but a box full of sincere surveys had to be reckoned with, and reckoning with sincerity requires a kind of energy that the

Evergreen Club had been conserving for exactly this sort of occasion.

"I've put together a short member satisfaction survey," Shelley said.

She said "short" the way real estate agents say "cozy," with the understanding that the word is doing more work than its definition supports.

The survey was four pages long. Four pages are not short for a survey. Four pages is a commitment. Four pages is the length of a survey designed by a person who believes that understanding a thing requires asking the thing sixty-three questions about itself, and that the sixty-three answers will assemble into a portrait that is more accurate than the thing would have produced if left to describe itself in its own words, which it was not being asked to do, because its own words were not standardized and the Department required standardization because standardization is how departments turn rooms into data and data into reports and reports into evidence that the department is performing its function, which is the production of reports.

Shelley distributed the surveys with the efficient warmth of a flight attendant distributing customs forms, the kind of distribution that implies participation is expected but not technically mandatory, except that the plane is in the air and you are on it and the form is in your hand and the alternative to filling it out is explaining to a uniformed person why you chose not to, and the explanation will take longer than the form.

Each survey was stapled in the upper left corner. The staple was precise. The paper was bright white, the kind of white that suggests the document was printed that morning and has not yet encountered the world's tendency to soften, crumple, and stain everything it touches. The paper was optimistic in the way only a paper that has never been used can be.

The first page was headed MEMBER SATISFAC-TION SURVEY in the Department's institutional font, followed by the subtitle: "Your feedback helps us serve you better!"

The exclamation point was doing a tremendous amount of work. It was the exclamation point of a sentence that knows it is not exciting but has been told to act excited, the way a child in a school play has been told to act like a tree, and the child is trying, and the effort is visible, and the visibility of the effort is the problem.

Below the subtitle was the instruction: "Please answer all questions honestly. Your responses are confidential and will be used to improve programming and services."

"Confidential," Twain said, reading the instruction the way a mechanic reads a dipstick, looking not at what the word says but at what it indicates. "Confidential means the answers go into a file. The file goes into a cabinet. The cabinet sits in an office. The office belongs to the Department. The Department reads the file when it needs to justify a decision it has already made. Confidential does not mean private. Confidential means the audience has been reduced, not eliminated."

"The responses are anonymized," Shelley said.

"Anonymous," Twain said. "In a club with nine members, two dogs, a cat, and a raven. Anonymous. As if the person who writes a twelve-page addendum to a four-page survey could possibly be anyone other than Dickens. As if the person who answers every question with a refer-ence to ice could be anyone other than Melville. Anony-mous. In this room. That is not anonymity. That is a costume party where everyone comes dressed as themselves."

She printed a label. It read: ANONYMOUS (FICTIONAL).

I looked at my copy of the survey. The questions began on page two, and they began with the kind of question that surveys always begin with, which is a question so broad that answering it honestly would require either a single word or an autobiography, and the survey wanted neither. The survey wanted a number.

Question 1: On a scale of 1 to 10, how satisfied are you with your overall experience at the Evergreen Club?

I stared at the question. I stared at it the way you stare at a door installed in a wall where no door is needed, a door that leads to a room you did not know existed and do not wish to enter, but which, now that the door is there, you cannot stop thinking about.

How satisfied was I with my overall experience at the Evergreen Club? The question assumed that the experience could be rated. The question assumed that satisfaction was a spectrum with ten positions and that my position on the spectrum could be identified and recorded and compared to the positions of other members, and the comparison would produce a number, and the number would mean something, and the something it meant would be useful to people who had never sat in the chair that has been through things and watched a raven decide not to speak.

What was the number for a room where an egg timer rings and nobody asks why? What was the number for a pineapple that presides? What was the number for the particular quality of silence that follows Austen resetting the timer, the silence that is not empty but full, full of the agreement that the people in this room have made with each other without ever stating it, which is the agreement to be here without being required to explain why being here is enough?

Seven? Was that a seven? Or was it the kind of experience that breaks the scale, not because it is extreme but because it is the wrong shape for the container? You cannot pour a room into a number. You cannot pour a pineapple into a scale of one to ten. The pineapple does not fit. The pineapple has never fit. The pineapple's refusal to fit is its entire contribution.

I wrote "7" because you have to write something, and seven is the number people write when they are satisfied but unwilling to commit to the enthusiasm implied by eight or the perfection implied by ten or the nihilism implied by anything below five. Seven is the number of private contentment. Seven is the number that says, "This works, and I do not need you to know how much."

Question 2: How valued do you feel as a member of the Evergreen Club? (1 = Not at all valued, 10 = Extremely valued)

Valued. The word sat on the page like a guest who has arrived at the wrong party and is too polite to leave. I did not come to the Evergreen Club to feel valued. I came to the Evergreen Club to sit in a chair, drink good ice, and watch a cat make poor decisions. "Valued" is a word that belongs in human resources departments and performance reviews, and the kind of conversation where a manager tells you that your contributions matter, and the fact that the manager has to tell you is the proof that the telling is the substitute for the mattering.

The Club did not make me feel valued. The Club made me feel present. Present is better than valued. Present is what you are when the room is not trying to make you anything. Present is the natural state of a person who has arrived somewhere and has not been asked to justify the arrival. Valued is what happens when someone notices you are present and decides to score it.

I wrote "8" because the question deserved a higher number than my objection to it.

Question 3: What activities would you most like to see added to the Evergreen Club? (Check all that apply.)

The options were:

☐ Chair yoga ☐ Art classes ☐ Book discussion groups
☐ Music appreciation ☐ Guest speakers
☐ Health and wellness workshops ☐ Technology training
☐ Cooking demonstrations ☐ Gardening
☐ Other (please specify): _______________

I looked at the list. The list was a menu of activities that someone who had never been to the Evergreen Club believed the Evergreen Club should offer, based on the assumption that older people in rooms want to do things that can be listed, and that the absence of listed things is the absence of things, and that the absence of things is a problem. The list did not include "sitting." The list did not include "being in a room." The list did not include "watching a raven not speak," or "listening to a man explain ice," or "allowing a cat to make the worst possible decision and learning from the aftermath." The list did not include the things the Club actually did because the things the Club actually did could not be listed because listing them would turn them into activities, and they were not activities. They were conditions. You cannot schedule a condition. You can only be in one.

I checked "Other" and wrote: "The Evergreen Club does not add activities. The Evergreen Club is the activity."

This was, I recognized, the kind of answer that would be useless to Shelley and the Department, and the uselessness was the point, because the survey was built to receive useful answers and useful answers were the raw material from which programs were constructed, and programs were the thing the Club existed to not be. Giving a useful answer to this survey was the same as giving the Department a brick; the Department would use it, and the building the Department built with the bricks would be the building the Club was moved into; the Club would not survive the move.

I looked around the room.

Dickens was writing. He had been writing since the survey was distributed, and he was not writing on the survey. He was writing on additional sheets of paper he had brought from home because Dickens had sensed that a survey was coming, the way some people sense the weather, and he had arrived prepared. He was on his fourth page. The handwriting was small, dense, and organized into sections with headers and subheaders, and, on the third page, what appeared to be a footnote system.

"The survey asks what activities I would like to see added," Dickens said, without looking up. "I have prepared a comprehensive response. I am recommending a twelve-session series on the history of infrastructure, with particular attention to sewage systems, bridge construction, and the development of postal routes. Each session would include a lecture, a discussion, a practical exercise, and a take home reading list. I have drafted the first three lecture outlines, and I am prepared to serve as the instructor, moderator, and administrator of the series. I will also need a whiteboard."

"You always need a whiteboard," I said.

"Whiteboards are the infrastructure of ideas. Without them, ideas have no surface. Without a surface, ideas cannot be shared. Without sharing, ideas remain private. And private ideas are the most dangerous kind because they grow without oversight."

He returned to his writing. His pen moved across the page with the relentless energy of a person who has never once been stopped by the realization that the thing he is producing exceeds the scope of the request. Dickens did not recognize scope. Scope was a limitation, and limitations were problems, and problems were things that could be solved with additional pages.

Twain had filled out seven copies of the survey.

She had taken the stack of blank surveys from the box when Shelley was not looking, which was a brief window because Shelley was almost always looking, but Shelley had been distracted by Dickens's fourth page and the distraction had created an opening and Twain had exploited the opening with the speed and precision of a person who had been planning this since the box arrived.

Each copy was filled out under a different name. The names were not real names. They were labels. The first survey was attributed to CONCERNED MEMBER. The second to ANONYMOUS DISSENTER. The third to THE PINEAPPLE (PROXY). The fourth to CHAIR #4 (SUPPORTIVE BUT JUDGMENTAL). The fifth to UNDISCLOSED. The sixth to CLASSIFIED. The seventh to THE EGG TIMER.

Each survey had different answers. CONCERNED MEMBER rated satisfaction at 6 and requested better lighting. ANONYMOUS DISSENTER rated satisfaction at 3 and requested the removal of all surveys. THE

PINEAPPLE (PROXY) rated satisfaction at 10 across every category and added no comments because the pineapple had no complaints, no suggestions, and no interest in the improvement of anything. CHAIR #4 (SUPPORTIVE BUT JUDGMENTAL) rated satisfaction at 7 but noted, in the comments section, that some members sit incorrectly and that posture is a form of communication. THE EGG TIMER rated satisfaction as "N/A (cyclical)" and requested that the question be reformulated to accommodate nonlinear experiences of time.

Twain arranged all seven surveys in a neat stack and placed them in the collection box that Shelley had set up near the door.

"This will compromise the data," I said.

"The data was compromised the moment it was collected," Twain said. "I have simply made the compromise visible. If nine people fill out a survey and sixteen surveys are returned, the Department must either acknowledge that the data is unreliable or accept that the Evergreen Club has more members than it knows about, and either conclusion is more honest than the conclusion they were going to draw from nine sincere responses filtered through a framework that was built before anyone in the Department had met us."

This was, I had to admit, the most coherent argument Twain had ever made about anything. It was also the most subversive thing anyone had done in the Club's history, more subversive than Melville's ice, more subversive than Austen's four-second silences, more subversive than the pineapple's refusal to explain itself. Twain had not resisted the survey. She had multiplied it. She had taken the Department's instrument and used it to produce noise, and noise was the enemy of data, and data was the weapon the

Department was using, and Twain had jammed the weapon by filling it with ammunition that did not fit.

I was, briefly, in awe.

Austen was filling out his survey with the methodical care of a person completing a tax form he philosophically opposes, but is unwilling to leave blank because leaving it blank would be an act of refusal, and refusal could be interpreted as defiance, which could be interpreted as instability, and instability was the justification for intervention. Austen did not refuse. Austen complied in a way that communicated the minimum possible information while technically satisfying every requirement, the way a prisoner of war gives name, rank, and serial number. His answers were complete. His answers were accurate. His answers told the Department nothing it could use, because Austen had spent a lifetime learning how to say things that were true and empty at the same time, and this skill, which in most contexts would be called evasion, was in this context a form of defense.

He rated his satisfaction at five across every question. Five was the center of the scale. Five was the number that says "I have answered" without saying anything else. Five was the number of a man who is cooperating with a process he does not recognize as legitimate and is giving the process exactly what it deserves, which is the mathematical middle, the place where enthusiasm and complaint cancel each other out and what remains is a flat, featureless plain of compliance that reveals nothing and costs nothing and gives the Department a number that cannot be argued with because it cannot be interpreted.

Woolf filled out her survey in a single unbroken paragraph that started in the response box for Question one, continued into the margins, then onto the back of the page, and then onto a second page, and then onto a third. The paragraph began with the survey and ended somewhere else entirely, somewhere that had to do with the nature of institutional measurement and the way that asking someone to quantify their experience was itself an experience and the experience of being quantified was different from the experience being quantified and the difference was the thing the survey could not measure because the survey was the thing creating the difference.

Her response to Question 1 began: "Satisfaction is not a number. Satisfaction is not even a word that means what it appears to mean. The word comes from the Latin *satis*, meaning enough, and *facere*, meaning to make or to do, so satisfaction is literally the making of enough, and the question is whether enough can be made or whether enough is a condition that arises without making, the way sleep arises, or hunger, or the particular feeling of standing in a room where nobody is asking you to be anything other than present, which is the feeling this survey is attempting to capture by asking me to assign it a value between one and ten, and the assignment is the destruction of the thing being assigned because the thing being assigned is precisely the experience of not being assigned anything..."

It continued for two thousand words. It was, by any reasonable standard, the most beautiful response to a member satisfaction survey ever written. It was also completely unusable as data, which made it the most useful thing Woolf had ever produced in the context of the Club's defense, because a response that cannot be entered into a spreadsheet is a response that cannot be used against the person who wrote it, and Woolf had written a response that would break any spreadsheet it was entered into, not through refusal but through excess, the way a river breaks a dam not by opposing it but by being more than it can hold.

Melville filled out his survey in four minutes. He rated satisfaction at nine for every question except Question 7, which asked: "How satisfied are you with the refreshments provided at meetings?" He rated this a 2.

In the comments section, he wrote: "The refreshments are adequate with the exception of the ice, which I provide myself because the Club does not have the correct ice, has never had the correct ice, and will not have the correct ice until it acquires a Scotsman SCN60 nugget ice machine, which produces sixty pounds of nugget ice per day at the correct compression ratio, and which I have researched extensively and can recommend without reservation. The ice currently available, if I do not bring my own, is freezer ice, which is ice in the way that a photograph of a sunset is a sunset, which is to say it is technically accurate and experientially false."

He added, at the bottom, in smaller handwriting: "The crackers are fine."

The Psychoanalyst did not fill out the survey. He analyzed it.

He sat in his chair, the most comfortable chair, the chair he had claimed at his first meeting and returned to at every subsequent meeting with the unerring accuracy of a homing pigeon who believes the coop was built specifically for him. He held the survey at arm's length and read it the way a doctor reads an X-ray, looking not at what was present but at what the presence revealed about the underlying structure.

"The survey itself is a projection," he announced. "Each question reveals more about the Department than it could ever reveal about the respondent. Question one asks about satisfaction, which tells us the Department is concerned with satisfaction, which tells us the Department is anxious about its own performance, which tells us the Department is projecting its anxiety onto the Club by asking the Club to measure what the Department fears it cannot provide. The survey is not a request for information. It is a confession."

"Fill out the survey," Austen said.

"I am engaging with the survey on a deeper level."

"Engage with it on the level that involves a pen."

The Psychoanalyst smiled, the smile of a man who has been asked to do something beneath him and is complying only because the request is itself more interesting than the task. He picked up a pen. He filled out each question with a 5, matching Austen's responses exactly, which was either coincidence or the Psychoanalyst's way of demonstrating that he could read people well enough to predict their answers, and the ambiguity between coincidence and demonstration was a space the Psychoanalyst was very comfortable occupying because ambiguity was his natural habitat, the way water is a fish's natural habitat, and asking the Psychoanalyst to leave ambiguity was like asking a fish to take a walk.

In the comments section, he wrote: "The Club does not need a survey. The Club needs to ask itself why it is afraid of being known."

It was the most irritating thing he had ever written, and it was in a competitive category.

Byron ate a survey.

This was not a metaphor. Byron, who had been circling the box of blank surveys with increasing interest since Shelley placed it near the door, reached into the box with one paw, extracted a single sheet from the middle of the stack with the surgical precision of a creature who has never once questioned his right to interfere with human processes, and began chewing on it.

He chewed methodically. He chewed the way cats chew paper, with a combination of aggression and boredom that suggests the paper has wronged them in a previous life and that the chewing is not hunger but justice. He reduced the first page to a damp, wrinkled rectangle of pulp. He moved to the second page. The second page contained Questions fifteen through thirty-two, including "How would you rate the Club's commitment to diversity and inclusion?" "Do you feel the Club adequately addresses the needs of differently-abled members?", and "Would you support the introduction of a Club newsletter?"

Byron chewed through all of them.

"Byron," Shelley said, reaching for the remains.

Byron looked at her with the expression of a cat who has been interrupted during something important and is deciding whether the interruption merits retaliation or merely contempt. He chose contempt, which is the cat's default response to everything that is not food, and sometimes also to food, depending on the food's willingness to be eaten on the cat's terms.

He dropped the shredded survey, walked to the pineapple, and sat beside it with the serene indifference of a creature who has just destroyed a document and considers the matter closed.

"He ate Question twenty-three," Shelley said, holding up the remains. "Question twenty-three was about the newsletter."

"The newsletter," Twain said, "has been reviewed."

Poe shifted on the curtain rod.

The shift was subtle. A redistribution of weight from one foot to the other. A tightening of feathers along the spine that made the raven look taller, more formal, the way a person looks when they stand slightly straighter because something in the room has reached the level of seriousness that their posture was waiting for.

Poe opened his beak.

The room was noisy. The room was always noisy during surveys because surveys produced opinions and opinions produced speech and speech produced more speech, and the cycle was self sustaining, a conversational engine that ran on disagreement and was cooled by nothing. Dickens was on his seventh page. Twain was printing labels for each of her seven proxy surveys. Melville was explaining the Scotsman SCN60's compression ratio to Steinbeck, who was listening with the patient devotion of a dog who has never once understood a word a human has said to him and has never once needed to. Woolf was still writing, her pen moving in long continuous strokes that suggested the paragraph had not ended and might never end, and the ending was not the point.

Nobody was watching Poe.

Nobody except me.

The beak opened wider this time. Wider than before. The throat moved, the same small muscular contraction, the same mechanical preparation. But this time there was something behind it, a pressure, a sound building in the chest the way a sound builds in a pipe organ before the key is fully depressed, the air moving but not yet released, the note forming but not yet sounding.

I leaned forward in my chair.

Poe's eye caught mine. The eye was black, the kind of black that is not an absence of color but a presence of something that color cannot describe, the black of a creature that has watched centuries of human noise and has distilled it all into a single sound that has not yet been spoken because the sound is waiting for the room to be ready, and the room was not ready, and the raven knew it, and the raven closed his beak.

The sound retreated. Whatever it was, wherever it was going, it went back inside, and Poe settled on the curtain rod with the patience of a creature that has all the time in the world because time is a human invention and the raven was here before the humans and will be here after, and the word, whatever the word is, will keep.

The surveys were collected at the end of the meeting. Shelley gathered them from the collection box with the careful hands of a person handling something she believes will be useful. She counted them. She counted sixteen. She looked at the stack. She looked at the room. She counted the members. She counted the surveys again.

"There are sixteen surveys," she said.

"The Club has diverse representation," Twain said.

"There are nine of you."

"Nine present. The others submitted remotely."

Shelley looked at the surveys. The top one was attributed to **THE EGG TIMER**. The one beneath it was attributed to **CHAIR #4 (SUPPORTIVE BUT JUDG-MENTAL)**. She opened her mouth to say something, then closed it. She put the surveys in her portfolio, which now had Byron's claw marks on the exterior, puncture holes on the interior, and a small smear of something that might have been cheese, or might have been a memory of cheese from a cracker that had not survived the meeting.

"Thank you for your participation," she said.

She said it with the professionalism of a person who knows the data is compromised and has decided to process it anyway because the alternative is admitting that the process itself was inadequate, and admitting the process was inadequate is the one thing a person who believes in process cannot do.

She left.

The room was quiet.

The box of remaining blank surveys sat by the door. Byron had returned to it and was sleeping on top of it, which was his way of ensuring that no further surveys left the box without his approval. His approval was not forthcoming, and the box was warm; the warmth was enough.

Austen looked at the pineapple. The pineapple had not been surveyed. The pineapple's satisfaction had not been measured. The pineapple existed outside the Department's instruments, the way it existed outside everything, completely, totally, and without apology.

"Same time next week," Austen said.

The egg timer rang.

He did not reset it.

The not-resetting was the answer to a question nobody had asked, which is the Club's preferred method of communication, and which no survey will ever capture, and which is why the Club works, and which is why the Department will never understand it, and which is why the pineapple presides, and which is why the raven has not yet spoken, and which is why the ice is good, and which is why the chairs are trained, and which is why I come back every week and sit in the chair that has been through things and wait for the timer to ring and the timer to be reset and the silence after the reset to fill with the particular nothing that the Evergreen Club has made into everything it needs.

I went home. Steinbeck walked beside me. Hemingway walked ahead.

At the desk, I did not write anything. Some evenings,

the correct response to a survey about your satisfaction is to refuse to evaluate your satisfaction and instead sit in a room with two dogs and acknowledge that the room is enough and the dogs are enough and the refusal is enough and the word for all of it is a number that does not exist on any scale from one to ten.

I assigned it a seven anyway, privately, in my head, because seven is the number of a man who knows the scale is wrong but fills it out anyway, and filling it out anyway is how you survive institutions, and surviving institutions is how you keep the room, and keeping the room is everything.

Chapter 6

THE BOARD

The formation of the board of directors was announced at the next meeting with the quiet inevitability of a thing that everyone knew was coming and no one had been able to prevent, the way a dentist appointment arrives on the calendar and you have known about it for six months and you have had six months to cancel it and you did not cancel it because canceling it would require a phone call and the phone call would require an explanation and the explanation would require you to admit that you are avoiding something, and admitting you are avoiding something is worse than the thing itself, so you go to the appointment and you sit in the chair and the chair reclines and the light comes on and you open your mouth because the alternative is to keep it closed and keeping it closed is not an option the chair was designed for.

Shelley had prepared a document. The document was titled EVERGREEN CLUB BOARD OF DIRECTORS: FORMATION AND GOVERNANCE FRAMEWORK.

It was nine pages long, which was three pages longer than the grant application's governance section, which suggested that Shelley had added material, which suggested that Shelley had been thinking about this, which suggested that Shelley thought about the Club when she was not at the Club, which was the most concerning development since the brochure because a person who thinks about you when you are not present is a person who is building something, and the thing they are building does not require your participation to continue being built.

The document had sections. The sections had subsections. The subsections had bullet points, and the bullet points had the clean, purposeful energy of ammunition arranged in a magazine, each one ready to be deployed in sequence toward a target that the bullet points collectively defined, which was the conversion of the Evergreen Club from a room into an organization.

"The grant requires a minimum board of five members," Shelley said. "I've drafted a proposed structure."

She handed out copies. The copies were warm from the printer, which meant she had printed them that morning, which meant the document had been finalized recently, which meant there had been a draft, which meant there had been revisions, which meant multiple people at the Department had looked at this document and agreed that it was the correct way to organize a room that contained a pineapple, two dogs, a cat, a raven, a bag of fast food ice, an egg timer that measured nothing, a thousand-piece puzzle with one confirmed corner, a label maker, and a fluorescent work light that was currently unplugged and leaning against the wall like a decommissioned weapon.

The proposed board structure was:

Chair: Shelley (Community Enrichment Liaison, Department Representative) Vice Chair: To Be Determined (Club Member) Secretary: Austen (Host) Treasurer: To Be Determined (Club Member) At-Large Member (Under 40): To Be Determined (Intergenerational Representative)

I read the structure twice. The first time I read it was for content. The second time I read it for what the content revealed, which was a different thing, the way reading a menu tells you what a restaurant serves, and reading the prices tells you what the restaurant thinks of you.

Shelley had placed herself as Chair. This was not a hostile act. It was not even, in Shelley's understanding, a presumptuous act. It was a logical act. Shelley was the liaison. Shelley represented the Department. The Department was providing the funding. The funding required oversight. Oversight required a chair. Shelley was the chair. The logic was clean, sequential, and entirely correct if you accepted the premise, which was that the person providing the money should govern how the money was used, and the person governing how the money was used should sit at the top of the structure, and the structure should have a top, and having a top was natural, and natural meant correct.

The logic was also the logic of every institution that has ever arrived in a room full of people who were doing fine and rearranged the room so that the institution was in the center and the people were around it, and the people were told this was support.

Austen had been assigned the role of Secretary. Secretary. The man who had built the room, who had selected the furniture, who had established the principle that the chairs should be trained and the pineapple should preside and the egg timer should ring without explanation, the man who opened the door before you knocked and reset the timer without checking the dial and assessed your gravity within three seconds of your arrival, this man had been assigned the role of taking notes.

The Secretary role is the one you give to a person when you want to acknowledge their presence without acknowledging their authority. The Secretary is the title that says, "You are important enough to be in the room but not important enough to decide what happens in it." The Secretary is the organizational equivalent of being seated at a dinner party near the kitchen, close enough to hear the conversation, yet far enough to understand that you are not expected to lead it.

Austen read the document. He read it once, completely, without expression, the way a judge reads a brief before rendering a decision that has already been made internally but must be processed publicly for the record. His face did not change. His posture did not change. The pen in his hand did not move. The only indication that he had finished reading was that he set the document down on the table next to the pineapple and aligned it with the edge of the table so precisely that the alignment itself was a statement, because Austen communicated through precision, and the precision with which he handled the document was the precision of a man who is taking a thing seriously enough to destroy it methodically rather than emotionally.

"Secretary," he said.

He said it once. He did not need to say it again. The word sat in the room and the room heard it and the room understood everything the word contained, which was not just a title but a demotion, not just a demotion but a misunderstanding, not just a misunderstanding but the specific kind of misunderstanding that occurs when a person who has never built anything is given authority over a person who has built everything, and the authority is structural and the building was personal and the structure does not recognize the personal because the structure was not designed to recognize it. The structure was designed to organize, and organizing is what you do to things that you believe cannot organize themselves, and the belief that the Club cannot organize itself is the belief that made the brochure and the survey and the grant and now the board, and the board is the final step, the step where the belief becomes architecture and the architecture becomes permanent and the people inside the architecture become inhabitants of someone else's design.

"The Secretary role is vital," Shelley said, with the encouraging tone of a person who has sensed that something has gone wrong but has not yet identified what. "The Secretary maintains the official record. Minutes, correspondence, documentation. It's the backbone of governance."

"The backbone of governance," Austen repeated, "is not the record. The backbone of governance is the judgment that determines what is worth recording. A secretary records what others decide. I do not record. I decide. I have always decided. The door opens because I open it. The timer resets because I reset it. The pineapple presides because I placed it, and I maintain it, and I have never once, in the history of this Club, asked anyone's permission to do so. I am not the backbone. I am the spine."

Shelley wrote something in her notebook. I could not see what she wrote but I could see the speed of the writing, which was fast, which meant she was recording rather than considering, which meant the words would be reviewed later in an office where the context would be absent and the words would stand alone and the words alone, without the room and the timer and the pineapple and the particular quality of Austen's voice when he says something that matters, would read differently from how they sounded. Words always read differently from how they sound. This is why minutes are dangerous. Minutes are the ghost of a conversation. They have the shape but not the warmth.

"Austen," I said, "does not need a title. Austen is the title."

"For the purposes of the grant," Shelley said, "every board member needs a formal role."

"For the purposes of the room," I said, "Austen is the host. Host is the role. Host encompasses every function that the board is created to distribute among five people. You are taking a single person who performs a complex, unified function and dividing that function into five titles that will perform it worse because division is not the same as delegation. Division is what you do to a thing when you do not trust the thing to remain whole. Austen has remained whole. The Club has remained whole. The wholeness is the thing you are about to break into a five-person committee, and the committee will spend its time reassembling what did not need to be disassembled."

Shelley looked at me with the expression of a person who is hearing an argument that she recognizes as coherent but cannot accommodate because accommodating it would mean abandoning the structure she has built, and the structure is her job, and her job is her identity, and her identity is the thing that tells her she is helping, and being told she is not helping is the same as being told she is not herself, and nobody can process that standing up in a room full of strangers while a cat chews on their portfolio.

"The structure is required by the grant," she said.

"The structure is required by the grant," Austen agreed. "And the grant is required by the Department. And the Department is required by the budget committee. And the budget committee is required by the political process. And the political process is required by the voters. And none of them, not one, from the grant to the voter, has ever been in this room or seen this pineapple or heard this timer ring or watched this raven sit on this curtain rod and decide, with the full weight of whatever ancient authority a raven possesses, that the room is acceptable as it is."

He looked at Poe. Poe looked back. The exchange lasted less than a second but carried more governance than the nine-page document on the table.

Dickens had been reading the governance framework with the focused intensity of a man who has been handed a blueprint and cannot help but admire the engineering even as he disagrees with the building. "The committee structure is interesting," he said. "There are provisions for standing committees, ad hoc committees, and advisory panels. I could work with this. I could improve it. The standing committee structure, for instance, could be expanded to include a Programming Committee, a Facilities Committee, an Outreach Committee, and a Committee on Committees to coordinate the other committees."

"Dickens," Austen said.

"I am only saying that if we must have a board, we should have the most thorough board possible. Half measures produce half results. If the Department wants governance, we should give them governance so complete that it takes them six months to read the minutes."

This was, by Dickens's standards, a subversive idea, possibly the second most subversive idea Dickens had ever produced, after the blank section titled "Regarding the Pineapple." The idea was not to resist the board but to overwhelm it. To create a governance structure so dense, so layered, so thoroughly documented that the Department would drown in its own requirements. It was a strategy of excess. Compliance as a weapon. Paperwork as warfare.

Austen considered this. You could see the consideration in the slight tilt of his head, the way a chess player tilts when a move has been suggested that is inelegant but effective.

"No," he said. "We will not out govern them. Out governing them still accepts their premise. The premise is that governance is necessary. We do not accept the premise. We accept the seat."

He turned to Shelley. "I will serve as Secretary," he said. "I will keep the record. The record will be accurate. The record will be complete. The record will contain everything that happens in this room as I observe it, and nothing that happens in this room as the Department imagines it, and the difference between those two records will be the space in which the Club continues to exist."

He said it with the calm of a man accepting a lesser title the way a general accepts a diplomatic post, not because the post reflects his rank but because the post provides access to the room where the decisions are made, and access to the room is worth more than the title on the door.

Shelley nodded, relieved. The relief was visible. She had expected more resistance to the Secretary role and had received a sentence that sounded like acceptance, and she did not hear the architecture inside the acceptance, the way you do not hear the foundation beneath a house, but the foundation is there and the house is the foundation's idea of what a house should be, and Austen's acceptance was a foundation that Shelley had not designed and could not see and would not discover until the building was occupied and behaving in ways the blueprint did not predict.

"For Vice Chair," Shelley said, "I'd recommend one of the longer-standing members. Someone with institutional knowledge."

"Institutional knowledge," I said. "In a club with no institution."

"Organizational memory, then."

"The organizational memory of this Club is the pineapple, and the pineapple does not attend meetings. The pineapple is the meeting."

Dickens raised his hand. "I would be willing to serve as Vice Chair," he said. "I have experience with organizational structures. I have designed seventeen committee frameworks in the last three years, twelve of which were implemented and five of which are still pending review by committees that have not yet been formed, but which I am confident will be formed once the framework for their formation has been approved by the committee I intend to propose at the first board meeting."

The room absorbed this.

"Dickens would be an excellent Vice Chair," Austen said, and he said it with the particular tone of a man who is making a strategic appointment, because Dickens as Vice Chair would produce so much documentation that the board would never have time to do anything except read Dickens's documentation, and a board that is reading is a board that is not governing, and a board that is not governing is a board that exists on paper and nowhere else, which was exactly where Austen wanted it.

"Wonderful," Shelley said. She checked a box on her document. The check was small, precise, and satisfactory.

Each checked box was a step toward the structure she believed in, and the steps were accumulating, and the accumulation felt like progress, and progress felt like proof that the help was helping.

"For Treasurer," she said.

"What funds require a treasurer?" Austen asked.

"The grant funds. Someone needs to oversee the budget, approve expenditures, and maintain financial records."

"The grant funds belong to the Department. The Department disperses them according to the approved budget. The Treasurer would be overseeing money that is not ours, held in accounts we do not control, disbursed according to rules we did not write. The Treasurer would not be managing our money. The Treasurer would be managing their money while sitting in our room."

"It's a fiduciary responsibility," Shelley said.

"It is a fiduciary performance," Austen said. "The Treasurer performs the role of financial oversight the way a scarecrow performs the role of a farmer. The form is present. The function is elsewhere."

Melville raised his hand. "I will be Treasurer," he said.

The room looked at him.

"The Scotsman SCN60 is an eligible facility improvement," he said. "If I am Treasurer, I can ensure the budget includes the Scotsman SCN60. I can prioritize the Scotsman SCN60. I can protect the Scotsman SCN60 from budget reallocation. The Scotsman SCN60 will have an advocate in the financial structure, and the financial structure will have a Treasurer who understands the only expenditure that matters."

"Melville," Austen said.

"I understand the conflict of interest. I accept the

conflict of interest. The conflict of interest is the reason for the position. Every Treasurer in history has had a conflict of interest. The conflict is the interest. Without the conflict, the position is clerical. With the conflict, the position is meaningful. I will be the most meaningful Treasurer this Club has ever had."

"This Club has never had a Treasurer."

"Then I will be the first and the most meaningful. Both records, one appointment."

Austen looked at Melville for a long moment. The look was the look of a man who is watching an ally walk toward the enemy camp with a white flag in one hand and a bag of ice in the other, and the man is not sure whether the ally is surrendering or conducting a negotiation that only the ally understands, and the uncertainty is the thing that makes the alliance valuable, because an ally whose strategy you can predict is an ally whose strategy the enemy can also predict, and Melville's strategy was unpredictable because Melville's strategy was always and only about ice, and ice is the last thing any opponent prepares for.

"Melville will be Treasurer," Austen said.

Shelley checked another box. Two boxes in five minutes. The structure was assembling itself with the momentum of a thing that has been planned and is now simply being revealed, the way a building is revealed when the scaffolding comes down, and the scaffolding was Shelley's patience and the building was the board and the board was becoming real in the way that things become real when enough people agree to act as though they are real, which is the only way anything has ever become real.

"The At-Large Member under forty," Shelley said. "This is the intergenerational requirement. Do any of your members have a family member or community contact under forty who might be interested in serving?"

The room was quiet.

The room was quiet because nobody in the room had a family member or community contact under forty who might be interested in serving on the board of a club that met weekly in an unregistered room to not explain a pineapple. The members of the Evergreen Club had children and grandchildren and nieces and nephews, but those children and grandchildren and nieces and nephews had their own rooms and their own pineapples and their own egg timers, and the egg timers of the young do not ring the way the egg timers of the old ring, and the young do not hear the ring when it comes because the young have not yet learned to listen for it.

"I can identify a candidate from the Department's volunteer pool," Shelley said.

"A stranger," Austen said.

"A community member."

"A stranger sent by the Department to sit on our board and represent a generation that is not present in our room because our room is not for that generation, not because we exclude them, but because they have not yet arrived at the place in time where this room makes sense, and placing them here before they arrive is not intergenerational engagement. It is casting. It is filling a role that the script requires and the story does not."

"The grant requires it."

"The grant requires many things. The grant requires a board, and we are forming a board. The grant requires a treasurer, and we have appointed a man whose fiscal policy is ice. The grant requires a secretary, and you have made the host into a clerk. The grant requires intergenerational representation, and you will send us a young person who will sit in this room and not know why the timer rings, and not know why the pineapple is here, and not know that the correct response to both mysteries is silence, because silence is not taught. Silence is earned. And this room is full of people who have earned it."

Byron jumped onto the table. Byron had been unusually quiet during the board discussion, which in retrospect should have been a warning, because Byron's quiet periods were not periods of rest. They were periods of planning, the way a thunderstorm does not begin with thunder. It begins with stillness.

Byron walked across the governance framework. His paws left no marks because the paper was thick, but the walk itself was a mark, a physical crossing of a document that claimed authority over a room that Byron considered his territory. He walked from the first page to the last page, pausing on page five to sit on the section titled **RESPONSI-BILITIES OF THE CHAIR**, which he kneaded twice with his claws before continuing.

He reached the end of the document and sat on the signature line.

"Byron," Shelley said.

Byron looked at her. Byron looked at the room. Byron looked at the pineapple, his associate, his fellow resident of the central table, the only other entity in the room that did not need to explain itself.

And then Byron did the thing that Byron did best, which was the thing nobody expected because Byron operated outside the framework of expectation, the way weather operates outside the framework of scheduling. Byron curled up on the signature line, tucked his tail over his nose, and went to sleep.

The signature line now read, in Shelley's neat handwriting, AT-LARGE MEMBER (UNDER 40), and on top of those words was a small orange cat who was under forty, under four in fact, and who had placed himself in the intergenerational seat with the serene confidence of a creature who had never once considered the possibility that he did not belong exactly where he was.

"The position," Twain said, reaching for her label maker, "appears to have been filled."

She printed a label. She placed it on the table next to Byron. It read: BOARD MEMBER (SELF-APPOINTED, UNDER 40, INTERGENERATIONAL, NON-NEGOTIABLE).

Shelley looked at the cat. Shelley looked at the document. Shelley looked at the room, which looked back at her with the collective expression of people who have watched a cat solve a bureaucratic problem and see no reason to improve on the solution.

"The position requires a human representative," Shelley said.

"The position requires an under-forty representative," Twain said. "The document does not specify species. I have read it. The word 'human' does not appear. The word 'person' does not appear. The word 'individual' appears once, in the context of individual responsibility, and Byron is an individual, and Byron has demonstrated responsibility by showing up to every meeting and consistently refusing to respect institutional authority, which is exactly the kind of oversight a board needs."

"A cat cannot serve on a board of directors."

"A cat," Twain said, "already does."

This was the moment when Shelley should have laughed. This was the moment when a different kind of person would have recognized that the room was telling her something through comedy that it could not tell her through argument, and the thing the room was telling her was that the board was a fiction and the Club knew it was a fiction and the Club was willing to participate in the fiction as long as the fiction did not take itself seriously, and a cat on the signature line was the Club's way of saying "we will play your game but we will not pretend it is not a game."

Shelley did not laugh. Shelley wrote something in her notebook. The something she wrote was probably a note to identify a human candidate from the volunteer pool, and the human candidate would arrive at the next meeting and sit in a chair and not understand the timer and not understand the pineapple and not understand why a cat had claimed their seat, and the not understanding would be permanent because understanding the Evergreen Club required time, and time was the one thing the grant's structure did not provide, because the grant measured time in quarters and the Club measured time in egg timer intervals that corresponded to nothing and meant everything.

Austen looked at the completed board. Chair: Shelley. Vice Chair: Dickens. Secretary: Austen. Treasurer: Melville. At-Large Member: to be determined by the Department, though Byron had filed a counter-claim.

"The board is formed," Shelley said.

She said it the way a person says "the surgery is complete," with the satisfaction of someone who has performed a procedure and believes the patient will be better for it. The patient was the Club. The Club had not requested surgery. The Club had been operating without surgery for its entire life and, by its own assessment, had been functional. But the Department had looked at the Club and seen a patient, and once you are seen as a patient, the surgery becomes inevitable, because the only thing a surgeon cannot do is look at a body and decide it does not need to be opened.

"The first board meeting will be next Thursday," Shelley said. "I'll prepare an agenda."

"We have never had an agenda," Austen said.

"Every board meeting requires an agenda."

"Every meeting at the Evergreen Club has required only a pineapple and an egg timer."

"The agenda formalizes the discussion."

"The discussion," Austen said, "was never informal. It was simply not written down. There is a difference between informal and unrecorded. Informal means without structure. Unrecorded means without evidence. We have always had structure. Our structure is the timer, the pineapple, the host, and the room. What we have never had is evidence, and the absence of evidence is not the absence of governance. It is the presence of trust. Trust does not require an agenda. Trust requires only that the people in the room have agreed, without documents, without signatures, without a board, to be in the room and to let the room be what it is."

Shelley put the document in her portfolio. The portfolio was increasingly battered. Byron's punctures, the survey residue, and now the governance framework had all been placed inside it, and the portfolio was becoming a record of its own, a physical history of the campaign to formalize the Evergreen Club, told not in the documents it contained but in the damage it had sustained while containing them.

"Same time next week," Austen said.

Shelley smiled. "Same time Thursday," she corrected. "For the board meeting."

Austen did not correct the correction. He let it stand.

He let it stand the way a man lets a crack in a wall stand, not because the crack is acceptable, but because pointing at the crack does not fix it, and fixing it requires tools he has not yet assembled.

The egg timer rang.

Austen reset it. He reset it with the same motion he always used, the motion of a man who has performed this action so many times that the action is no longer a task but a reflex, and the reflex is no longer a habit but a principle, and the principle is the thing that the board cannot govern because the board does not know it exists.

The interval began.

I went home. Steinbeck walked beside me. Hemingway walked ahead. At the desk, I looked at the growing collection. The four-sentence letter. The brochure with Twain's labels. The survey with my sevens. And now the board, which existed on paper and which would exist in practice next Thursday and which would continue to exist as long as the grant existed and the grant would exist as long as the Department existed and the Department would exist as long as departments exist, which is to say forever, because departments are the one human invention that has achieved immortality, not through accomplishment but through the simple refusal to conclude.

Hemingway sat by the door. He had opinions about the board. His opinions were positional. He was between the room and the outside, and the outside now included a Chair, a Vice Chair, a Secretary, a Treasurer, and a pending intergenerational representative, and all of them would have to pass through the door, and the door was Hemingway's jurisdiction, and Hemingway's jurisdiction did not recognize the authority of boards, only the authority of the ground he occupied, and the ground was his, and the ground would remain his regardless of what the agenda said.

Steinbeck was asleep. Steinbeck's response to governance was the same as his response to weather, crisis, surveys, and brochures: trust, followed by sleep, followed by more trust. It was not a strategy. It was a constitution. And constitutions, unlike boards, do not require agendas.

Chapter 7

THE PROGRAMMING

The programming began on a Monday because Mondays are the day institutions choose when they want to establish authority over a week. Friday would be too lenient. Wednesday would be too democratic. Monday is the day that says "we are beginning something and the beginning is not optional," the day that arrives with the administrative weight of a door being opened by someone who has keys you did not give them.

Shelley had prepared a schedule. The schedule was laminated, which is the institutional equivalent of carving something in stone. Lamination says this is permanent. Lamination says this has been approved. Lamination says the conversation about whether this should exist has ended and the conversation about how it will be implemented has begun, and you were not consulted about the transition between those two conversations because the transition happened in an office you have never been to, during a meeting you were not invited to, and the lamination is the proof that the meeting occurred and the proof is waterproof.

The laminated schedule read:

EVERGREEN CLUB WEEKLY PROGRAMMING Monday: Wellness Hour (10:00 AM - 11:00 AM) Wednesday: Creative Expression (10:00 AM - 11:00 AM) Friday: Community Dialogue (10:00 AM - 11:00 AM)

Below the schedule was the Department's tree logo, which had acquired a third element since the brochure. The tree now stood beside a small river, and the river was flowing in a direction that rivers do not flow, which was upward, as if the designer had added the river without consulting the river about the physics of being a river, and the river had complied because the designer had the software and the river did not.

Shelley had also prepared supplies. The supplies arrived in three separate boxes, one for each day of programming, and the boxes were labeled with the Department's labeling system, which was not Twain's labeling system, and the difference between the two labeling systems was the difference between a language that had grown organically from within a room and a language that had been applied from outside a room, and the difference was legible to everyone in the Club and invisible to everyone in the Department.

Twain looked at the Department's labels with the expression of a person who has been shown a counterfeit of her own currency. She did not touch them. She did not relabel them. She stood at a distance and studied them the way a painter studies a forgery of her work, noting where the lines were close and where they were wrong and understanding that the closeness was worse than the wrongness because closeness implied imitation and imitation implied that the original could be replaced, and Twain's labels could not be replaced because Twain's labels were not information. They were opinion. And opinion, unlike information, cannot be standardized.

"They have labels," she said.

"They have labels," Austen confirmed.

"Their labels are incorrect."

"Their labels are the Department's labels."

"That is what I said. Incorrect."

She reached for her label maker. She did not relabel the Department's boxes. She labeled the space beside them. She placed a label on the table that read: DEPARTMENT LABELS (NOT ENDORSED). She placed a second label on the wall behind the boxes that read: CONTENTS UNDER EXTERNAL AUTHORITY. She placed a third label on her own label maker that read: STILL THE STANDARD.

The coexistence of two labeling systems in one room was, for Twain, a constitutional crisis. It was the presence of a competing government on sovereign soil. She would tolerate it because Austen asked her to tolerate it, and she would tolerate it the way nations tolerate embassies: she acknowledged their existence without recognizing their authority and reserved the right to apply her own labels to any surface she considered part of her jurisdiction, which was every surface, including the surfaces the Department believed it controlled.

The first Wellness Hour, on the first Monday, was led by a woman named Harper. Harper was not a member of the Club. Harper was a contractor provided by the Department, a certified wellness facilitator whose certification hung on a lanyard around her neck and whose qualifications included, according to the laminated bio Shelley distributed, "fifteen years of experience in holistic health coaching, mindfulness instruction, and senior wellness programming."

Harper was approximately thirty-five. She had the bright, centered energy of a person who begins each morning with a practice, ends each evening with a reflection, and fills the hours between with the systematic application of wellness to people who have not requested it. She wore yoga pants and a fleece vest and shoes that were designed for a lifestyle, not a task, shoes that communicated not "I am going somewhere" but "I have arrived at a state of being and the state of being is comfortable."

"Good morning, everyone," Harper said, with the voice of a person who has been trained to project warmth the way a radiator projects heat, mechanically, efficiently, and in all directions, regardless of whether the room is cold. "I'm so excited to be here. Today we're going to start with some gentle chair yoga, move into a guided breathing exercise, and finish with a group wellness check-in."

She said "wellness check-in" as if the words were a gift she was unwrapping in front of them.

The room received this information the way it received all external information, which was with a silence that communicated not hostility but assessment, the silence of people who have been alive long enough to know that the first five minutes of any new arrangement tell you everything you need to know about the next five years.

"Chair yoga," Austen said.

"Yes. Very gentle. No equipment needed. Just your chair and your willingness to explore your body's relationship with movement."

"My body's relationship with movement," Austen said, "is professional. We have worked together for many years. We do not need couples counseling."

Harper laughed. It was the laugh of a person who has been trained to laugh at client resistance because laughter defuses resistance, and the training was visible in the laugh, the way training is always visible when it replaces instinct.

"That's a great attitude," she said. "Let's start with some seated stretches. Everyone, if you could push your chairs back from the table just a bit."

Nobody pushed their chairs back from the table. The chairs at the Evergreen Club were positioned as they were positioned because the positions had been established over time through a process of incremental adjustment that reflected each member's relationship to the room, to the table, to the pineapple, and to each other. The chairs were not furniture. They were territories. Asking a member of the Evergreen Club to push their chair back was like asking a country to move its border. The request was technically possible and practically an act of war.

"I will not be moving my chair," Austen said. "My chair is where my chair is."

"Mine is also where it is," I said. "It has been through things. I do not rearrange it without consultation."

"My chair," the Psychoanalyst said, from the most comfortable chair, which he had claimed with the same inevitable gravity that pulls a river downhill, "is positioned to allow optimal observation of group dynamics. Moving it would compromise my sight lines."

"You do not need sight lines," I said. "You are not a sniper."

"Observation is its own form of precision."

"Your precision is unwelcome."

"The unwelcomeness confirms its accuracy."

Harper looked at Shelley. Shelley looked at Harper. Between them passed the brief, encrypted communication of two professionals who have encountered a room that is not cooperating with the protocol and must decide in real time whether to adapt the protocol to the room or the room to the protocol, and the decision is always the same because the protocol is the thing that justifies their presence and adapting the protocol is the same as admitting the protocol is wrong and admitting the protocol is wrong is the same as admitting the presence is unnecessary.

"Let's try the stretches in place," Harper said, adapting the protocol to the minimum amount required to avoid a standoff. "Just where you are. Raise your arms overhead. Gently. Like you're reaching for something on a high shelf."

Dickens raised his arms with the enthusiasm of a man who has been given a task and intends to complete it with distinction. He reached for the ceiling with both hands, fingers extended, body leaning, as if the high shelf were real and the thing on it were the missing corner pieces of his puzzle, and reaching for them were the most important thing he would do all day.

"That's wonderful," Harper said. "Now hold that stretch."

"I can hold it longer," Dickens said. "I can hold it for the duration of the session. I can hold it and work on the puzzle at the same time. Multitasking builds neural pathways."

"Just a gentle hold is fine."

Dickens held the stretch with competitive intensity. He held it the way he did everything, as if the activity had a score and the score had a leaderboard, and the leaderboard would eventually be published in a document he would file in the appropriate committee's records.

Woolf did not raise her arms. Woolf was sitting by the window, which had become her permanent station since the first meeting, the place where the light came in, and the room met the outside, and the boundary between the two was visible in the way the curtain moved. She was watching Harper the way she watched everything, from slightly outside the event, as if the event were a painting and she were standing in the gallery, close enough to see the brush-strokes but far enough to see the frame.

"The body does not need to be told to stretch," Woolf said, without raising her arms. "The body stretches when it wakes. It stretches when it has been still too long. It stretches when the mind forgets to hold it in position, and the muscles remember what the mind has overridden. The body's relationship with movement is not something you explore. It is something you stop preventing. Telling the body to stretch is like telling water to flow. The water already knows. The instruction is for the instructor, not the water."

Harper processed this. You could see the processing in the slight tilt of her head, the brief recalibration of a person whose training has prepared her for resistance but not for philosophy, and the difference between resistance and philosophy is the difference between a wall and a window, and you can push through a wall but you can only look through a window, and Woolf was a window.

"That's a beautiful perspective," Harper said, which is what wellness professionals say when they encounter some-thing they cannot categorize and need a moment to recover.

"It is not a perspective," Woolf said. "It is a description."

Melville had positioned his bag of ice on the table and was performing the stretches with one hand while keeping the other hand on the bag, as if the bag required physical contact to maintain its integrity, or as if letting go of the bag during a structured activity was a form of institutional capitulation that he was not prepared to perform. He reached for the ceiling with his right arm. His left arm remained on the ice. The asymmetry was striking, the image of a man divided between compliance and conviction, reaching upward with half his body and holding on with the other half, and the holding on was the half that mattered.

"You can use both arms," Harper said gently.

"I cannot," Melville said.

"Is there a physical limitation?"

"The limitation is the ice."

Harper looked at the bag. The bag looked back at her with the neutral indifference of a thing that does not know it is an obstacle but has become one through the sheer force of someone's devotion to it. Harper had been trained in adaptive wellness, in modifying exercises for physical constraints, for mobility limitations, for chronic conditions, and recovery protocols. She had not been trained for ice.

"Perhaps you could set the ice down for just a moment," she said.

Melville looked at her with the expression of a man who has been asked to set down something that cannot be set down, not because it is heavy, but because setting it down would mean it is optional, and the ice was not optional. The ice was the foundation. The ice was the first principle. You do not set down your first principle during chair yoga. You hold it tighter.

"The ice stays," Melville said.

"The ice stays," Austen confirmed from across the room, performing the role of Secretary by recording a decision that had not been voted on and did not need to be because some decisions are made by the room and the room does not vote. The room knows.

Harper moved on to guided breathing. The guided breathing involved closing your eyes, which Austen would not do because Austen did not close his eyes during organized activities as a matter of governance. It involved breathing in through the nose for four counts, which Hemingway did instinctively because Hemingway breathed the way he did everything, with controlled, deliberate intake followed by a pause that was not relaxation but assessment. It involved breathing out through the mouth for six counts, which Poe observed from the curtain rod with the air of a creature who had been breathing successfully for years without a guide and was not impressed by the formalization of a process that nature had already perfected.

"Feel the breath moving through your body," Harper said. "Notice where you hold tension. Your shoulders. Your jaw. Your lower back. Breathe into those spaces."

"You cannot breathe into your lower back," the Psychoanalyst said, eyes open, analyzing Harper with the same penetrating focus he applied to everyone. "The lungs do not extend to the lumbar region. What you are describing is a visualization technique, not a respiratory event. The instruction is metaphorical, but it is presented as literal, and the gap between the metaphor and the literal is the space in which wellness culture operates, which is the space between what is true and what feels true, and what feels true is the product you are selling."

Harper opened her eyes. "I'm not selling anything," she said.

"Everyone is selling something. You are selling the feeling of wellness. The feeling of wellness is not wellness. The feeling is the product. The wellness is the branding."

"He does this," I said to Harper, because someone always needed to say it, and the duty rotated. "To everyone. It is not personal."

"It is observation," the Psychoanalyst said.

"Your observation," Woolf said from the window, "is a performance of observation. You observe the way a mirror reflects. Accurately, automatically, and without understanding what it is showing."

The Psychoanalyst paused. Woolf had done it again. She had matched him with a sentence that was both a compliment and a dismantling, and the precision of it left him with nowhere to go except the word he always went to.

"Fascinating," he said.

"Predictable," Woolf replied, and turned back to the window.

The wellness check-in at the end of the hour required each member to share one word that described their current state. This was the kind of exercise that wellness facilitators use to "take the temperature of the room," which is a phrase that assumes the room has a temperature and the temperature can be measured and the measurement will be useful, and none of these assumptions are valid in a room where the egg timer measures nothing and the pineapple presides and the raven has not spoken.

"One word," Harper said. "Just one word that captures how you're feeling right now."

"Functional," Austen said.

"Industrious," Dickens said.

"Labeled," Twain said.

"Hydrated," Melville said.

"Observed," Woolf said.

"Illuminated," the Psychoanalyst said, and he meant it therapeutically, and the room received it with the particular weariness of people who have heard someone use the word "illuminated" about themselves and know that the illumination is self-administered and self-congratulatory and will not be dimming anytime soon.

"Present," I said, because present was the truth and the truth was one word and one word was all the exercise deserved.

Steinbeck wagged his tail, which was not a word but was an answer.

Hemingway did not participate. Hemingway's one word, if he had been able to provide it, would have been 'positional,' and 'positional' is not a feeling. It is a strategy. But Hemingway did not distinguish between the two, and the lack of distinction was his greatest strength.

Byron, who had slept through the entire Wellness Hour on top of the pineapple, stretched, yawned, and knocked a puzzle piece off the table. This was his one word. His one word was chaos, and chaos does not need to be spoken. Chaos announces itself through action and then goes back to sleep.

Wednesday was Creative Expression.

Creative Expression was led by Shelley herself, because the Department's budget had not included a second contractor for midweek programming and Shelley had volunteered, which was the kind of volunteering that occurs when a person believes their enthusiasm is a qualification and their qualification is enthusiasm, and the two together produce a session that is organized, earnest, and missing the point in a way that only earnest organization can achieve.

Shelley arrived with supplies. She had also brought a pineapple upside down cake, which she had called "Shelley's Monster Cake." She had baked it herself, at home, the night before, and she carried it in a glass dish covered with foil, and she placed it on the snack table beside the crackers with the careful pride of a person presenting something that had required effort and eggs and a recipe she had looked up on her phone while the oven preheated. The cake was golden and caramelized and the pineapple rings on top were arranged in the pattern that pineapple rings are always arranged in on pineapple upside down cakes, a circle of rings around a center ring, and the symmetry was decorative and the cherries were red and the cake smelled like butter and brown sugar and the particular optimism of a person who believes that a room can be reached through its stomach.

Nobody ate it.

Nobody refused it. Nobody said anything about it. Nobody looked at it with hostility, suspicion, or even a visible decision. The cake simply sat on the snack table beside the crackers and the mixed nuts, and the members moved around it the way water moves around a stone in a stream, not with resistance but with the fluid, automatic adjustment of people whose path to the crackers did not include the cake and whose path would not be rerouted by its presence. The pineapple upside down cake sat twelve inches from the pineapple that sat on the center table, one less organized and the two pineapples occupied the same room the way a portrait occupies the same room as the person it was painted from, one real and one interpreted, one unexplained and one caramelized, one presiding and one cooling, and the one that was cooling would still be there at the end of the session, untouched, and Shelley would carry it home in the same glass dish with the foil replaced, and she would not mention it, and the room would not mention it, and the not mentioning was the room's answer to the cake the way silence is the answer to a question that was never wrong but was never the right question.

The supplies Shelley" brought included colored pencils, watercolor sets, blank paper, magazines for collage, glue sticks, scissors, and a stack of "creative prompts" printed on index cards. The index cards were color-coded. The color-coding corresponded to a system that Shelley had developed and that nobody in the room would use because the room already had a color-coding system, and the system was Twain's labels, and introducing a second color-coding system into Twain's territory was like introducing a second sun into a solar system. The orbits would not hold.

"Today," Shelley said, "we're going to explore our inner creative voices through visual art."

"My inner creative voice," Twain said, "expresses itself through labels. My inner creative voice does not require colored pencils. My inner creative voice requires a Brother P-Touch PT-D210 label maker with TZe tape and a fresh set of AAA batteries."

"Labels can absolutely be part of your creative expression," Shelley said, with the accommodating warmth of a person who has decided to include rather than redirect, and the inclusion was genuine and the warmth was genuine and the decision to treat label-making as a creative art form was the moment Shelley came closest to understanding the Club, though she did not know it, because the closest you can come to understanding the Club is to accept that the people in it are already doing the thing you are asking them to do, they are just doing it in a language you do not speak.

Twain nodded, satisfied, and began creating labels. She created labels for the art supplies. She created labels for the creative prompts. She labeled each colored pencil with its Pantone number, which she knew from memory because

Twain's memory for classification systems was photographic, and her need to apply classification systems to unclassified objects was medical.

Dickens took the watercolors and the blank paper and immediately began painting, not a picture but a diagram. The diagram was a flowchart of the creative process as he understood it, beginning with "Inspiration" and flowing through "Ideation," "Planning," "Execution," "Revision," "Committee Review," "Subcommittee Approval," and "Final Publication," with arrows connecting each stage and footnotes explaining the governance of each transition. It was the least creative piece of art ever produced in a session called Creative Expression, and it was the most Dickens thing Dickens had ever done, and Dickens was very pleased with it.

"This is my process," he said, holding up the flowchart, which was dripping watercolors in a way that made the arrows bleed into each other, giving the entire diagram the unintentional appearance of a thing that was falling apart while insisting it had structure. "I wanted to share my process because process is the art. The product is secondary. What matters is the system."

"That is a beautiful reflection on process," Shelley said, and she meant it, or she meant the sentence, or she meant the act of saying the sentence, and the distinction between those three things was the distinction between understanding and accommodation, and Shelley was always accommodating, and accommodation was her art, and her art was never going to be enough because accommodation without understanding is decoration, and decoration is what the brochure was, and the brochure was the beginning of the problem.

Woolf had been given a blank sheet of paper and a set

of colored pencils. She had placed the colored pencils in a row along the windowsill, arranged by spectrum, and had been staring at them for twenty minutes. She had not drawn anything. She had not picked up a pencil. She was looking at the colors the way she looked at everything, as if the colors were not objects but states, and the states were not fixed but moving, and the movement was the thing she was trying to see, not the color itself but the way the color changed when the light changed, and the light was always changing, and so the color was always becoming a different color, and drawing a color that was always becoming a different color would be a lie because the drawing would fix the color and the color refused to be fixed.

"Would you like a prompt?" Shelley asked, offering an index card.

Woolf looked at the card. The card was blue. The prompt read: "Draw a place that makes you feel safe."

Woolf held the card for a long time. She held it the way you hold a sentence you are trying to understand, not as language but as intention, reading not the words but the assumptions behind the words. A place that makes you feel safe. The prompt assumed that safety was a place. The prompt assumed that the place could be drawn. The prompt assumed that drawing the place would be an act of expression rather than an act of reduction, that the drawing would capture the safety rather than flatten it into a shape that looks like safety but is only the memory of the shape of the feeling of the beginning of the thing that was never really a place at all.

"I do not have a place that makes me feel safe," Woolf said. "I have moments. Moments are not places. Moments cannot be drawn. They can only be noticed, and the noticing changes them, and the changed moment is not the moment that was safe. It is the moment after the safe moment, which is the moment of knowing you were safe, and knowing you were safe is not the same as being safe, because knowing introduces the possibility of not knowing, and not knowing is the end of safety."

She put the card down. She picked up a yellow pencil. She drew a single, horizontal line across the center of the page. Then she put the pencil down and went back to looking at the window.

The single line was the most honest piece of art produced in the session. It was a horizon. It was the line between the known and the unknown. It was the line the Club was standing on, the line between what the Club was and what the Department wanted it to become, and the line was thin and the line was yellow and the line was Woolf's answer to every question the Department had ever asked, which was: there is a boundary, and the boundary is here, and I have drawn it, and I will not explain it.

Melville painted the ice. He painted the ice realistically, with attention to its translucence, its irregular edges, and the way the light passed through the nuggets and scattered on the other side. He used every blue and white in the watercolor set. He mixed colors on the palette with the focus of a man who has spent years studying the subject and is finally being asked to represent it, and the representation was faithful, and the faithfulness was the thing that made it art rather than illustration, because faithful representation of a thing you love is always art, even when the thing you love is ice from a fast food chain.

"This is beautiful," Shelley said, looking at Melville's painting.

"This is accurate," Melville corrected. "Beauty is a

secondary effect of accuracy. If you represent the ice correctly, the beauty takes care of itself."

Friday was Community Dialogue.

Community Dialogue was the session that Austen had feared most because Community Dialogue required dialogue, and dialogue required topics, and topics required someone to select them, and the person selecting them was Shelley, and Shelley's topics were the Department's topics, and the Department's topics were the topics that departments always choose, which are topics that sound important and feel progressive and produce the kind of conversation that can be summarized in a quarterly report without anyone at the Department having to admit that the conversation did not go the way the summary suggests.

The topic for the first Community Dialogue was: "What Does Community Mean to You?"

Shelley wrote this on a whiteboard she had brought. The whiteboard was small, portable, and mounted on a tripod. The tripod stood at the front of the room, which was a room that did not have a front because the room was organized around the pineapple, and the pineapple was in the center, and the center is not the front, and putting a whiteboard at the front of a room that does not have a front is like putting a podium in a park. The podium creates the front, and the front creates the audience, and the audience creates the performance, and the performance is the thing the Club was built to avoid.

Dickens spoke first. Dickens always spoke first in structured discussions because structured discussions were his natural environment, the way water is a fish's natural environment, and Dickens, in a structured discussion, was a fish in water, entirely in his element and incapable of understanding why everyone around him was drowning.

"Community," Dickens said, "is the project of belonging. It is what happens when individuals agree to contribute to something larger than themselves. Community is built. It requires effort. It requires participation. It requires committees."

"Not everything requires committees," I said.

"Name one thing that does not benefit from a committee."

"Solitude."

"Solitude benefits from a committee dedicated to ensuring the conditions for solitude are maintained. Someone must manage the silence. Someone must protect the space. Someone must file the paperwork that guarantees the solitude will not be interrupted by people who want to form a committee about it."

He paused, realizing he had argued himself into a circle. He did not seem troubled by this. Dickens was never troubled by circles. Circles were just structures that hadn't found their corners yet.

Melville spoke about community as a shared resource. "Community is the agreement that we will all use the same ice," he said. "Not literally. But the principle is the same. Community means we have agreed on a standard, and that standard is maintained by the people who care about it most, and the people who care about it most are not the majority. The majority does not care about the standard. The majority accepts whatever ice is in the freezer. The community is sustained by the minority who carry the good ice from the source and refuse to let the standard drop."

"That is the most specific and least transferable definition of community I have ever heard," I said.

"It transfers perfectly," Melville said. "Replace ice with anything. Replace ice with justice. Replace ice with truth.

Replace ice with the thing you believe in more than the people around you believe in it. The person who carries that thing to the room every week, who does not trust the room to provide it, who brings their own because the room's version is not good enough, that person is the community. Without that person, the room has only what the room was given, and what the room was given was never enough."

The room was quiet. Melville had accidentally said something profound. He did not notice. He was adjusting his bag of ice.

Woolf spoke about community as the space between people, not the connection but the distance, and the quality of the distance, and the way the distance changes when the people inside it change, and the way the people change when the distance is the right distance, which is the distance where you can see the other person clearly without being close enough to distort them with your own expectations.

The Psychoanalyst spoke about community as a defense against mortality, because the Psychoanalyst spoke about everything as a defense against mortality, and mortality was the Psychoanalyst's pineapple, the thing at the center of every conversation he had ever had, the thing he could not stop explaining, the thing that presided over his every observation, and his inability to leave it alone was his defining quality and his greatest limitation and the reason that everything he said was almost right, which remained the most tiring kind of wrong.

Twain did not speak. Twain labeled. She labeled the whiteboard. She labeled the topic. She labeled each person's contribution as they spoke. Dickens: STRUCTURAL. Melville: DEVOTIONAL. Woolf: SPATIAL. The Psychoanalyst: TERMINAL. By the end of the session, the whiteboard was covered not in dialogue but in Twain's taxonomy of the dialogue, and the taxonomy was more informative than the dialogue itself, because the taxonomy said what the dialogue meant without requiring anyone to have meant it.

At the end of Friday, after three days of programming, after chair yoga and creative expression and community dialogue, after Harper and Shelley and the whiteboard and the watercolors and the prompts and the one-word check-ins and the breathing exercises, the room exhaled.

Not literally. Literally, the room had been breathing all week, guided and unguided, nasal and oral, four counts in and six counts out. But the room exhaled, as rooms do when the pressure is removed, and returned to what it is without being asked to be what someone else imagines it should be.

Austen removed the laminated schedule from the wall. He placed it face down on the table. He did not tear it. He did not discard it. He placed it face down, which is the action of a person who is not destroying a thing but putting it to sleep; the sleep may be temporary or permanent, and the distinction is not yet decided, and the not-deciding is itself a decision.

He reset the egg timer.

The timer rang.

He reset it again.

The room nodded.

The pineapple presided.

Byron climbed onto the overturned schedule and sat on it with the weight of a small creature who does not know he is making a statement and does not care, and whose not caring is the statement.

Poe watched from the curtain rod. Poe had watched the

entire week. Three days of programming. Three days of structured activities in an unstructured room. Three days of a room being asked to perform a version of itself that it did not recognize, the way a person is asked to perform a version of themselves in a job interview that bears no resemblance to the person they will be once they are hired.

Poe had watched Harper lead stretches. Poe had watched Shelley distribute prompts. Poe had watched the whiteboard appear at the front of a room that did not have a front. Poe had watched all of it with the patience of a creature that does not intervene because intervention is a human compulsion, and the raven's compulsion is witnessing, and witnessing is the harder thing because witnessing requires you to see what is happening and not change it and trust that the room will find its way back to itself without your help.

The room found its way back.

The room always finds its way back.

That is what rooms do, when you let them.

Chapter 8

THE INSPECTION

The inspector arrived on a Wednesday, which violated the schedule because Wednesday was Creative Expression, and the inspector was neither creative nor expressive. He was a man in a gray suit with a clipboard and a lanyard that identified him as Regional Program Evaluator, which is a title that means a person has been sent to determine whether a thing that exists should continue to exist, and the determination will be based on criteria that were written before the person saw the thing, and the criteria will not be revised after the person sees the thing, because criteria do not revise. Criteria persist. That is what makes them criteria.

His name, according to the lanyard, was Bennett.

Bennett entered the Club the way an auditor enters a business, with the professional neutrality of a person who has been trained to see everything and approve of nothing until the paperwork confirms that approval is warranted. He did not smile. He did not, not smile. His face occupied the precise midpoint between warmth and assessment, the face of a man who has learned that expressing an opinion before the evaluation is complete is a procedural error, and Bennett did not make procedural errors. Bennett made observations. The observations were recorded on the clipboard. The clipboard was the record. The record was the product. The product would be delivered to the Department, and the Department would read the product, and the product would determine whether the Evergreen Club qualified for the grant, and the grant would determine whether the Club was formalized, and the formalization would determine whether the pineapple remained a pineapple or became a logo.

Austen opened the door before Bennett knocked, maintaining the three-second protocol even under inspection conditions. This was not defiance. This was discipline. The door opened on Austen's terms regardless of who was on the other side, because the terms were the Club's terms and the Club's terms did not adjust for visitors, even visitors with clipboards, even visitors whose clipboards would determine the Club's future. Especially those visitors. The three-second protocol was never more important than when the person on the other side of the door believed they were the one granting entry.

"Welcome," Austen said.

He said "welcome" the way a sovereign says it to a diplomat. The word was warm. The posture was warm. The implication was not.

"Thank you," Bennett said, and looked past Austen into the room with the quick, cataloguing gaze of a person whose job is to convert spaces into assessments and assessments into recommendations and recommendations into decisions that affect people who were not consulted about the assessment.

Shelley was already inside, arranging the room, which

was the first problem. Shelley had arrived an hour early to prepare for the inspection, and preparing for the inspection meant rearranging the room so it looked like what the Department expected a community enrichment space to look like, which was different from what the room actually looked like, which was different from what the room was. Shelley had moved chairs into a semicircle facing the whiteboard because a semicircle suggests engagement and a whiteboard suggests programming, and the combination of the two suggests an organization that is doing things, and doing things was the thing the Department funded, and the Department's inspector was here to confirm that things were being done.

The semicircle was wrong. The chairs at the Evergreen Club did not form a semicircle. The chairs at the Evergreen Club existed in the positions their occupants had established through weeks and months and years of sitting in them, positions that reflected not an organizational chart but a gravitational field, with the pineapple at the center and each chair at the distance and angle that its occupant had negotiated with the room. Moving the chairs into a semicircle was like rearranging the planets into a line. The geometry was possible. The physics was not. The moment the members arrived, the semicircle would fail because people do not sit in the positions assigned by the furniture arrangement. People sit in positions assigned by who they are, and who they are is not a semicircle.

"The chairs have been moved," Austen said.

"I thought a semicircle would be more welcoming for the evaluation," Shelley said.

"The chairs do not form a semicircle. The chairs form the Club. The Club is not a semicircle. The Club is a room where each person has found the place where they can be in the room without being in anyone else's room, and the finding took time, and the time is the thing you have just undone by moving my chair six feet to the left."

He moved his chair back. He moved it to its exact previous position, with the spatial memory of a person who knows where everything in a room belongs, because the belonging is his responsibility, and the responsibility is his identity.

Steinbeck walked to where my chair should have been and sat down on the empty floor, waiting. Dogs do not care about furniture. Dogs care about locations. The location was correct. The chair would follow. Steinbeck trusted this with the same bottomless faith that he trusted everything, which was completely, and which was never wrong, because the world consistently rewarded Steinbeck's trust, which was either evidence that the world is fundamentally good or evidence that Steinbeck was fundamentally undemanding, and the distinction did not matter to Steinbeck because Steinbeck did not make distinctions. Steinbeck made himself available, and the world responded by being adequate.

I moved my chair back to where Steinbeck was sitting. Steinbeck wagged his tail. The universe was in order.

Hemingway had positioned himself between Bennett and the rest of the room, not blocking the entrance but occupying the space that a person would need to pass through to reach the interior, the way a checkpoint occupies a road. Hemingway was not aggressive. Hemingway was present. His presence was the message, and the message was: you may enter, but I have noted your entry, and my notes are not on a clipboard. My notes are in my posture, and my posture does not change based on your credentials.

Bennett looked at Hemingway.

Hemingway looked at Bennett.

The evaluation had already begun, and the evaluator was not the one with the clipboard.

The other members arrived, and each of them performed the same correction Austen had performed, moving their chairs from Shelley's semicircle back to the positions the room recognized. Dickens moved his chair and immediately resumed the puzzle, which had progressed to approximately eleven percent completion, the eleven percent representing the border, one confirmed corner, a section of what was definitively a barn, and a cluster of green that might have been a tree or might have been a different barn or might have been the puzzle's way of reminding everyone that eleven percent was not enough to be certain about anything. Twain moved her chair and placed a label on its back that read: **ORIGINAL POSITION (RESTORED)**. Melville moved his chair and adjusted the ice cooler to its standard orientation relative to the pineapple. Woolf did not move her chair because Shelley had not moved Woolf's chair, because Woolf's chair was by the window, and the window was not part of the semicircle because the window was Woolf's territory, and even Shelley, whose willingness to rearrange was institutional, had sensed that the window was not available.

The Psychoanalyst had arrived early enough to reclaim the most comfortable chair before Shelley moved it. He was already sitting in it when the semicircle was being formed, and Shelley had arranged the semicircle around him, the way a road is built around a boulder that is too large to move. He sat in the center of the former semicircle, like a monument forced to accommodate the renovation.

Bennett walked through the room. He walked slowly. He walked with the measured pace of a person who has

been trained to observe before he records and record before
he concludes and conclude before he recommends, and the
sequence was sacred to Bennett, and the sacred sequence
was what made him dangerous, because a person who
follows a sequence cannot be reasoned with. You can
reason with a person who is making a judgment. You
cannot reason with a process.

He looked at the walls. The walls were beige. The beige
had been chosen by Austen with the full weight of governance, the beige that said nothing and meant everything,
the beige that was the color of a room that refused to have
an opinion about its own appearance because having an
opinion about your own appearance invites other people's
opinions about your appearance, and other people's opinions are the beginning of renovation, and renovation is the
beginning of losing the room.

Bennett wrote something on his clipboard. The writing
was small and precise. The pen was a ballpoint, black ink,
institutional. The pen did not pause between words, which
meant Bennett was recording what he saw without
processing what it meant, and the recording without
processing was the most efficient and the most dangerous
way to observe a room, because the processing would
happen later, in the office, without the room, and the room
would not be there to correct the record.

He looked at the snack table. Shelley had upgraded the
snack table for the inspection. The crackers were a better
brand. The cheese was identifiable. The mixed nuts had
been replaced with a trail mix that included dried cranber-
ries and dark chocolate pieces, which elevated the snack
table from "obligation" to "effort," and the effort was visible, and the visibility of the effort was the point, because

inspections are not about what is. Inspections are about what is seen.

Melville's ice cooler was on the snack table. Bennett looked at it.

"Refreshment station?" he asked, writing.

"Ice station," Melville corrected.

"Is the ice provided by the organization?"

"The ice is provided by me."

"You personally provide the ice?"

"I personally procure, transport, and maintain the ice. The ice is from a Sonic Drive-In on Fourth Street. The one near the overpass. Not the one near the mall. The distinction is critical, and I am prepared to explain why if you have approximately forty-five minutes."

Bennett looked at Melville. Bennett looked at the cooler. Bennett looked at his clipboard. He wrote something. He did not ask for the forty-five-minute explanation, which was either professional restraint or survival instinct, and in Bennett's case, the two were probably the same thing.

He looked at the puzzle. "Activity station?" he wrote.

"Ongoing project," Dickens said, standing up with the eagerness of a man who has been asked about his work and considers every question about his work an invitation to deliver the full history of his work. "It is a thousand piece puzzle depicting a pastoral landscape. We are currently at eleven percent completion. The border is complete. One corner has been confirmed. The barn is taking shape. The sky remains entirely unsorted, which I attribute to the manufacturer's decision to use seventeen indistinguishable shades of blue, which I believe was an act of deliberate cruelty disguised as artistic ambition."

"How long has the puzzle been in progress?" Bennett asked.

"Since the Club's second meeting last year."

"How many meetings ago was that?"

Dickens calculated. The calculation involved counting backward through weeks, which involved counting backward through meetings, which involved remembering each meeting, which involved remembering what had happened at each meeting, which was a process that, for Dickens, was not calculation but narration, and narration for Dickens was never brief.

"The puzzle has been in progress for approximately seven months," he said. "At the current rate of assembly, accounting for the difficulty of the sky section, the seasonal variation in member attendance, and the periodic loss of pieces to Byron, I estimate completion in approximately fourteen additional months, plus or minus a quarter, depending on whether we locate the remaining three corner pieces, which I believe are in Byron's territory, which is the area beneath and behind the sofa, which is a region I have not yet been authorized to search."

Bennett wrote for a long time.

He looked at the labels. The labels were everywhere. Twain's labels had proliferated since the first meeting the way all living systems proliferate when the conditions are right, and the conditions in the Evergreen Club were always right for labels because the Club produced a continuous supply of things that required naming, and Twain's naming was faster than the Club's production, which meant Twain had begun labeling things that did not yet need labeling as a form of preventive taxonomy.

The spice rack was labeled. The chairs were labeled. The egg timer was labeled "TEMPORAL GOVERNANCE (AUTONOMOUS)." The pineapple's label, which Austen had forbidden and Twain had applied anyway during a brief interval when Austen was in the restroom, read: MANAGEMENT (DO NOT EXPLAIN). The label maker itself still read: ESSENTIAL PERSONNEL.

Bennett looked at the labels the way a person looks at graffiti in a museum, unsure whether it is vandalism or part of the exhibit.

"These labels," he said. "Are they part of the programming?"

"The labels are part of the room," Twain said. "The room has labels. The labels have a room. The relationship is mutual."

"Who authorizes the labels?"

"I authorize the labels."

"In what capacity?"

"In the capacity of the person who has the label maker."

·Bennett wrote this down. He wrote it down without expression, which was the most concerning kind of writing down because expressionless writing down meant the observation had been recorded without interpretation, and uninterpreted observations are the raw material from which any conclusion can be built, the way uncut stone is the raw material from which any sculpture can be carved, and the sculpture that the Department would carve from Bennett's observations would look like whatever the Department needed it to look like.

Shelley hovered near Bennett the way a real estate agent hovers near a potential buyer during an open house, close enough to narrate but far enough to allow the illusion of independent assessment. She pointed out the whiteboard. She pointed out the semicircle, which no longer existed because the chairs had returned to their true positions, but the ghost of the semicircle remained in Shelley's gestures, which traced an arc the room had rejected.

"As you can see," Shelley said, "the members are engaged in a variety of self directed activities. The puzzle is a long term collaborative project. The labels are a form of creative expression. The ice station provides refreshments. The programming schedule is posted."

She gestured toward the laminated schedule, which was face down on the table where Austen had placed it. Byron was sitting on it.

"It's posted," she said, with less certainty.

Bennett looked at the schedule. He looked at Byron. Byron looked at Bennett with the expression of a cat sitting on a piece of laminated paper who does not consider this remarkable and would like to know why you do.

"May I see the schedule?" Bennett asked.

"Byron," Shelley said.

Byron did not move. Byron's response to requests was the same as his response to gravity, physics, and institutional authority: to acknowledge their existence without accepting their jurisdiction. He had claimed the schedule. The schedule was beneath him, both literally and in every other sense. Moving would mean the schedule was more important than his position, and nothing was more important than Byron's position because Byron's position was Byron's primary creative output.

Shelley reached for the schedule. Byron placed one paw on her hand. The paw was gentle. The claws were not extended. But the message was clear. The schedule was occupied territory, and the territory was not being vacated on the authority of a lanyard.

"The cat," Bennett said, writing.

"The cat is Byron," Austen said. "Byron is a member of

the Club. Byron is also a member of the board of directors, pending a jurisdictional determination regarding species eligibility."

Bennett stopped writing. He looked at Austen. He looked at the cat. He looked at his clipboard. He looked at Shelley.

"The cat is on the board?" he said.

"The cat occupies the At-Large seat designated for members under forty," Austen said. "Byron is three years old. He meets the age requirement. The requirement does not specify species. This has been noted in the minutes."

"The minutes you keep as Secretary."

"The minutes I keep as Secretary are complete and accurate. They reflect everything that occurs in this room. If a cat sits on the board, the minutes record it. The minutes do not editorialize. The minutes are a mirror. If the mirror shows a cat on the board, the question is not whether the mirror is accurate. The question is whether the board was designed well enough to exclude a cat, and the answer, based on the documentation provided by the Department, is that it was not."

Bennett looked at his clipboard for a long time. He was encountering something his sequence had not prepared him for. The sequence was: observe, record, conclude, recommend. But the sequence assumed that the observations would be the kind of observations that lead to conclusions, and conclusions require categories, and Bennett's categories did not include a cat on a board of directors. The cat was outside the sequence. The cat was in the gap between the process and the room, and the gap was where the Club lived, and living in the gap was the Club's primary skill.

He moved on.

He looked at the pineapple.

Everyone in the room watched Bennett look at the pineapple. This was the moment. This was always the moment. The pineapple was the test. The pineapple sat in the center of the table with the same immovable authority it had always possessed, the authority of a thing that has never been asked to justify its presence because its presence is its justification. The pineapple was the Club. The Club was the pineapple. And the person looking at the pineapple was looking at the thing that would determine whether they understood, and understanding was not required, but the response to not understanding was the data point that mattered.

"The pineapple," Bennett said.

He said it the way you say the name of a thing you have encountered in a context where you did not expect to encounter it, the way you would say "elephant" if you opened your kitchen door and an elephant was standing there. The word was accurate. The word was insufficient. The word did not capture the pineapple any more than the word "elephant" would capture an elephant in your kitchen, because the thing that needs capturing is not the object. It is the presence of the object in a place where the object has no apparent reason to be, and the reason for its being there is the thing you are now required to either understand or accept, and understanding is not available, so acceptance is the only option, and acceptance without understanding is the definition of faith, and faith is the thing that institutions cannot evaluate because institutions evaluate evidence and faith is what you have when the evidence has run out.

"Yes," Austen said.

"What is it for?"

"It is a pineapple."

"Is it part of the programming?"

"It is not part of anything. It is the thing the parts are around."

Bennett wrote something. He wrote it slowly. The slowness suggested he was choosing his words, which meant the observation was not routine, which meant the pineapple had disrupted the sequence, which was the pineapple's function in every encounter with every external observer since the Club's founding. The pineapple disrupted by being. The pineapple did not need to do anything. The pineapple's existence was the disruption, because existence without explanation is the thing that processes cannot accommodate, and processes that cannot accommodate a thing must either ignore it or explain it, and ignoring it means it does not appear in the report, and explaining it means the report is wrong, and both outcomes protect the pineapple, and the pineapple knew this, or the pineapple was a pineapple and did not know anything, and the not knowing was itself the protection, and the protection was total.

"The brochure says it's a symbol of welcome," Bennett said.

"The brochure," Austen said, "was not written by anyone in this room."

"It describes your organization."

"It describes what the Department imagines our organization to be. The description and the organization are not the same thing. The map is not the territory. The brochure is not the Club. The pineapple is not a symbol of welcome. The pineapple presides. Presiding is not welcoming. Presiding is being present with authority, and the authority is not granted by a brochure, a grant, a board of directors, or a regional program evaluator. The authority is granted by the room, and the room granted it before any of you arrived, and the room will continue to grant it after all of you leave."

Poe dropped from the curtain rod.

He did not fly to the curtain rod or glide to the curtain rod. He dropped. He dropped to the back of the chair closest to Bennett, which was the chair next to mine, the chair that was empty because nobody sat in it and nobody had ever sat in it, and the emptiness of the chair was part of the room's arrangement, the way the silence between notes is part of a song. Poe landed on the back of the empty chair with the precision of a creature that has chosen its position the way a general chooses a hill, and the hill was chosen because it overlooked the battlefield, and the battlefield was Bennett's clipboard.

Bennett turned. Bennett was now face to face with a black raven at a distance of approximately eighteen inches. The raven was not hostile. The raven was not friendly. The raven was present in the way that ancient things are present, with the weight of every moment they have witnessed pressed into the stillness of the current one.

Poe cocked his head.

Bennett did not move. Bennett's training had prepared him for uncooperative members, hostile environments, incomplete documentation, missing records, and rooms that did not match their descriptions. Bennett's training had not prepared him for a raven studying him from the back of an empty chair with an expression that suggested the raven was conducting its own evaluation and the raven's evaluation was further along.

"The bird," Bennett said.

"Poe," Austen said.

"Is the bird part of the organization?"

"The bird is part of the room. Everything in this room is part of the room. The bird, the cat, the dogs, the pineapple, the timer, the ice, the labels, the puzzle, the chairs, the members. The room is not an organization that contains these things. The room is these things. You cannot evaluate the room by separating it into components because the components are not separate. The components are the room."

Poe stared at Bennett. Bennett stared at his clipboard. The clipboard offered no guidance. The clipboard was a tool designed for a world where things could be separated into components and the components could be evaluated individually, and the Evergreen Club was not that world, and the clipboard was failing, and the failure was quiet and total.

Bennett made a note. He underlined the note. The underlining was a decision, and the decision was that the note was important, and the importance would be communicated to the Department by the underlining, and the Department would read the underlined note and the Department would decide what the underlining meant, and the meaning would be whatever the Department needed it to mean, because underlining, like everything the Department did, was a tool of interpretation, and interpretation was the thing the Club could not control.

The inspection lasted forty-five minutes. Bennett looked at every surface. He counted chairs. He counted members. He did not count Byron, which was either an oversight or a jurisdictional decision. He asked about fire exits, accessibility, insurance, and liability. Austen answered every question with the precision of a man who has maintained a space to a standard that he set for himself, and that exceeds any standard an inspector could apply, because Austen's standard was not compliance. Austen's standard was dignity, and dignity encompasses compliance the way a cathedral encompasses a building code. The building code is met. The building code is not the point.

Bennett asked Shelley about the programming. Shelley described the programming with the polished enthusiasm of a person who has rehearsed her description and believes the description is accurate, and the description was accurate if you accepted the premise that the programming was programming, which the room did not accept but which the room did not contradict because contradicting the description during an inspection would be like contradicting the map during a navigation exercise. The map was wrong. The territory was right. But the person holding the map was the person deciding the route, and correcting the map would only produce a new map that was wrong in different ways.

The Psychoanalyst, to his credit, did not analyze Bennett. This was the most restrained the Psychoanalyst had been since joining the Club, and the restraint was not strategic. The restraint was instinctive. The Psychoanalyst had recognized Bennett as a fellow evaluator, and evaluators do not evaluate each other. Evaluators have a professional courtesy that prevents them from turning their instruments on their own kind, the way predators at a watering hole observe an unspoken truce. The Psychoanalyst and Bennett were both predators. The prey was the room. Neither predator would interfere with the other's hunt, even if the prey was the same.

The Psychoanalyst's only contribution was to tell Bennett, as Bennett was leaving, "The Club is more than it appears."

Bennett wrote this down. He did not ask what it meant. He did not need to ask. The sentence would appear in his report, and the report would not include the context, and without the context, the sentence could mean anything, and meaning anything was the Psychoanalyst's native language.

Bennett left at eleven-fifteen. He shook Austen's hand at the door. The handshake was professional. Bennett had come to evaluate. Bennett had evaluated. Bennett would write a report. The report would be filed. The filing would trigger a process. The process would produce a decision. The decision would determine the Club's future.

The Club's future was now in a clipboard carried by a man in a gray suit walking toward a sedan in the parking lot, and the sedan would carry the clipboard to an office, and the office would convert the clipboard into a document, and the document would be read by people who had never been in the room and never seen the pineapple and never heard the timer ring and never watched a raven decide that the back of an empty chair was the correct position from which to conduct a counter evaluation.

After Bennett left, the room exhaled for the second time in two weeks.

Poe flew from the empty chair back to the curtain rod. The flight was short, silent, and executed with the economy of a creature that has finished what it needed to do and is returning to its station, the way a sentry returns to a post after a patrol. The patrol had been successful. The sentry had been seen. The seeing was the point.

Austen reset the egg timer. The timer had not rung during the inspection. This was the first time in the Club's history that the timer had been silent during a meeting, and the silence of the timer was louder than the ringing had ever been, because the ringing was a ritual and the silence was an absence, and absence during an inspection meant the inspection had occupied the space the ritual usually filled, and the filling of that space by an inspector was the most concrete evidence yet that the Club was losing ground.

Austen reset the timer. The ring came. The room nodded. The ritual was restored. The restoration was not complete because restorations never are. Something had been in the room that did not belong there, and the room remembered, the way a body remembers a wound after it has healed. The scar is not the wound. The scar is the memory of the wound. And the Club now had a scar in the shape of a man with a clipboard who had looked at the pineapple and asked what it was for.

"He will recommend approval," Shelley said.

"How do you know?" I asked.

"He didn't find any disqualifying issues."

"He found a cat on the board of directors."

"He found an organization with engaged members, ongoing activities, and a unique culture."

"He found a room with a pineapple that nobody could explain."

"Unexplained things aren't disqualifying."

"Unexplained things," Austen said, quietly, from beside the timer, "are the only things worth qualifying for."

The room heard this. The room held it. The room would keep it the way rooms keep everything that matters, not in documents or minutes or quarterly reports, but in the quality of the silence that follows a sentence that has said the thing the room needed to hear.

Byron stretched on the laminated schedule, yawned with the full-bodied commitment of a creature who has never once apologized for taking up space, and went back to sleep.

The schedule remained face down.

The pineapple remained unexplained.

The egg timer ticked.

Shelley watched Bennett walk out with his clipboard. She looked pleased. She was watching a piece of the monster click into place, unaware of it. The room exhaled. The monster inhaled.

Chapter 9

THE INCIDENT

The incident began, as most incidents do, with a person trying to help.

Shelley arrived at the Thursday board meeting with a guest. The guest was the intergenerational representative the Department had selected to fill the At-Large seat that Byron had claimed and that the Department had declined to award to a cat despite Twain's documented argument that the governing framework did not specify species and despite Austen's minutes, which recorded Byron's self appointment with the same procedural neutrality that the minutes recorded everything, which was to say the minutes treated the cat's appointment and the Department's objection with equal weight because the minutes did not editorialize and the minutes did not take sides and the minutes were Austen's most precise instrument of resistance.

The guest's name was Parker. Parker was twenty-seven. Parker had a degree in nonprofit management and a minor in gerontology, which is a field that exists because someone decided that the experience of getting older was a subject that required study by people who had not yet gotten old, the way marine biology is the study of the ocean by people who live on land. Parker was earnest, prepared, and wearing a lanyard that said COMMUNITY VOLUN-TEER in a font that matched Shelley's lanyard, which meant Parker had been issued the lanyard by the Depart-ment, which meant Parker had been processed, which meant Parker was no longer a person who had volunteered. Parker was a credentialed volunteer, and credentialed volunteers are to actual volunteers what department ice is to Melville's ice, which is to say they share a name and a state of matter and nothing else.

Parker carried a tote bag. The tote bag said ENGAGE, ENRICH, EMPOWER. The tote bag was identical to Shelley's tote bag except that it had not yet been damaged by Byron, which meant it was new, which meant Parker was new, which meant the Department had given Parker a bag and a lanyard and a title and sent Parker into a room the Department had never understood and expected Parker to represent a generation the Department had decided needed representation without asking the generation or the room whether representation was the thing that was missing.

"Everyone," Shelley said, "this is Parker. Parker will be serving as our At-Large board member."

Byron was on the table. Byron had been on the table since before Parker arrived, sitting in his usual position beside the pineapple, occupying the space that he had occu-pied since the board was formed, the space that the minutes recorded as the At-Large seat. Byron looked at Parker the way a sitting tenant looks at someone who has arrived with a lease to the same apartment. The look was not hostile. The look was jurisdictional.

"Hi," Parker said. "I'm so excited to be here. I've read

the brochure and the programming schedule and the member satisfaction survey results, and I think what you all have here is really special."

Parker said "really special" the way young people say "really special" about things that older people have, which is with genuine admiration and the unconscious assumption that the admiration is a gift, and the gift is being given downward, from a person who has options to a person who has found one, and the finding is charming, and the charm is the thing the older person is supposed to be grateful for, and the older person is never grateful because the older person knows that what the young person calls special is what the older person calls Tuesday, and Tuesday does not require admiration. Tuesday requires only that you show up, sit in your chair, and wait for the egg timer to ring.

"Thank you," Austen said, which was the minimum response that hospitality permitted and the maximum response that the situation deserved.

"I've brought some ideas," Parker said.

Parker had brought ideas. The ideas were in a folder. The folder was organized with tabs. The tabs were color-coded. The color-coding was not Twain's color-coding. The introduction of a third color-coding system into a room that had already survived the introduction of a second color-coding system was an act of escalation that Twain registered with the quiet intensity of a person watching enemy troops cross a border they had been told was agreed upon.

"The first idea," Parker said, opening the folder with the bright, practiced confidence of a person who has given presentations before and has been told they are good at giving presentations and has believed the telling, "is a social media presence."

The room received this the way the room received all

new information, which was with a silence that was not empty but full of the things the silence was preventing people from saying.

"Social media," Austen said.

"An Instagram account. Maybe a Facebook page. We could document our activities, share photos of the members, highlight programming, and build community awareness. I've mocked up some sample posts."

Parker produced the sample posts. The sample posts were printed on glossy paper, each one showing a photograph that Parker had found somewhere, stock photographs of older people, different older people from the ones on the brochure, but produced by the same fundamental misunderstanding, which was that older people photographed in sunlit rooms doing organized activities was an image that represented something true about older people in rooms. The sample posts had captions. The captions included hashtags. The hashtags included #EvergreenClub, #SeniorCommunity, #AgingWithPurpose, and #VibrantLiving.

"Vibrant," Twain said.

"It's a strong brand word," Parker said.

"It is a word that has been applied to this Club by people who have never been in this Club, and it means the same thing every time it is applied, which is that the person using it believes we need a word to describe what we are because what we are is not enough without a word, and the word they have chosen is the word people use when they want to say 'old but still functioning,' which is not a compliment. It is a medical clearance."

Twain printed a label. The label read: #VIBRANT (UNAUTHORIZED).

Parker looked at the label. Parker looked at the sample

posts. Parker's face performed the small, rapid recalculation of a person whose presentation is not going the way the rehearsal suggested it would, and the recalculation was visible in the eyes, which were adjusting from "confident delivery" to "environmental assessment," which is the shift that occurs when a person realizes the room they are presenting to is not the room they prepared for.

"The second idea," Parker said, recovering with the resilience of a person whose training has included a module on managing resistant stakeholders, "is a mentorship program. Pairing Club members with younger community members for regular one-on-one conversations. Sharing wisdom. Building bridges across generations."

"Sharing wisdom," I said.

"Yes. Your members have so much to offer."

"We do. We offer a room with a pineapple and an egg timer. The wisdom is in the room. It is not extracted from us and distributed to younger people in a mentorship format. We are not mines. We do not have ore. We have experience, and experience is not transferable through a pairing program, because experience is not a substance. It is a condition. You cannot give someone your condition. You can only be in a room where the condition is visible, and if the younger person has the patience to sit in the room long enough, they will see the condition, and seeing the condition is the beginning of acquiring the condition, but the acquisition takes decades and cannot be accelerated by a program."

Parker wrote something in the folder. The writing was a reflex, the same reflex Shelley had, the note taking that converted conversation into data and data into plans and plans into the structure that would eventually replace the conversation that produced it.

"The third idea," Parker said, and here Parker paused, and the pause was the pause of a person who has saved their best idea for last and believes the best idea will win the room because the best idea is always the one the presenter is most excited about, and excitement is contagious, and contagious excitement overcomes resistance, and this belief is almost never true but is always held, "is a renovation."

The word landed.

"Renovation," Austen said.

He said it the way a person says the name of a disease they have been tested for and are now hearing confirmed. Not with surprise. With the recognition that the thing they feared was real, and the reality could no longer be managed by pretending it was still hypothetical.

"The grant includes funding for facility improvements," Parker said. "I've been looking at the space, and I think we could really open it up. New lighting. Updated furniture. A fresh paint scheme. Maybe a feature wall with the Club's mission statement. We could create a dedicated wellness corner, a creative station, a technology hub."

"A technology hub," Austen said.

"For the technology training programming. Tablets, maybe a smart TV for presentations. We could set up a charging station."

"A charging station. In a room where the primary technology is an egg timer."

"That's actually part of the charm we could highlight. The contrast between traditional and modern. The branding writes itself."

Austen stood up. Austen did not stand up during meetings. Austen sat. Sitting was his method of governance. Sitting was how he maintained the room, the way a captain maintains a ship by standing at the helm, except that Austen's helm was a chair and the chair was his authority and the authority was his stillness, and standing up was the abandonment of stillness, and the abandonment of stillness was the most alarming thing Austen had done since the Club's founding.

"The furniture," Austen said, standing, "is not going to be updated."

He said it quietly. The quiet was not calm. The quiet was the kind of quiet that precedes storms in places where storms are taken seriously, the quiet where the wind stops, and the birds stop, and the air becomes dense with the weight of what is about to happen.

"The furniture was selected. It was selected by me. Each piece was chosen for its capacity to support a person without judgment, to absorb the weight of a body that has carried itself for sixty or seventy or eighty years and needs a place to set the weight down without being asked to fill out a form about the experience. These chairs are trained. I have said this before. I will say it again. The chairs are trained. They know the people who sit in them. The people know the chairs. The relationship is not charming. It is not branding. It is the thing that the room is made of, and you cannot renovate the thing the room is made of without destroying the room."

He looked at the walls.

"The paint," he said, "will remain beige. Beige was chosen because beige does not participate. Beige does not assert. Beige does not inspire, depress, challenge, or comfort. Beige allows the room to be whatever the people in the room need it to be, which is different every day and different for every person and cannot be anticipated by a paint color, no matter how carefully the paint color has been selected by a person with a degree in nonprofit management and a minor in gerontology."

He looked at Parker. The look was not unkind. The look was the look of a man who sees a younger person making the mistake that younger people make: believing that the visible is the important, that the surface is the substance, that a room can be improved by changing what it looks like without understanding what it is.

"You mean well," Austen said. "You mean very well. The well-meaning is not in question. The well-meaning is never in question. The well-meaning is the most dangerous quality a person can bring into a room that is working, because the well-meaning does not see a room that is working. The well-meaning sees a room that could work better, and the 'better' is always the well-meaning person's idea of better, and the idea of better is always based on what is missing, and what is missing is always the thing the well-meaning person would have put there, and the thing the well-meaning person would have put there is always wrong, not because the thing is bad but because the thing displaces the nothing that was there before, and the nothing was the point."

He sat down.

The sitting down was the restoration. The standing had been the alarm. The sitting was the resolution. Austen was back in his chair. The chair received him the way it always received him, with the trained patience of a piece of furniture that had held this man through every crisis the Club had faced and would hold him through this one, because the chair had been through things and knew what it was for.

The room was quiet.

Parker was quiet. Parker's folder was closed. Parker's

sample posts were face down on the table. Parker's tote bag was at Parker's feet, and its message, ENGAGE, ENRICH, EMPOWER, faced the floor, which did not read it and did not care.

Then everything went wrong at once.

It went wrong the way things do in rooms full of people who care about different things, who have been under pressure for weeks, and who have been asked to accommodate a process they did not agree to while maintaining the dignity they did agree to. It went wrong not through a single failure but through a cascade of individual actions, each one reasonable in isolation, each one catastrophic in combination, each one taken by a person who was trying to solve the problem and instead added to the problem the way each drop of water added to a flood is, individually, just a drop.

Dickens started a committee.

He stood up, moved to the whiteboard that Shelley had left from the Community Dialogue session, and began writing. He wrote EMERGENCY RESPONSE COMMITTEE across the top in large letters, and beneath it, he began listing subcommittees. The subcommittees included: Subcommittee on Furniture Preservation, Subcommittee on Paint Color Continuity, Subcommittee on Pineapple Security, Subcommittee on Egg Timer Autonomy, and a Subcommittee on Subcommittee Coordination to ensure the other subcommittees did not overlap in jurisdiction.

"We need structure," Dickens said. "We need organized resistance. We need to formalize our informal objections so that the formal structure cannot dismiss them as merely informal."

"You are creating the thing we are resisting," I said.

"I am creating a better version of the thing we are

resisting. The only way to fight a structure is with a superior structure. You cannot oppose a committee with a feeling. You oppose a committee with a better committee."

"You oppose a committee by not being a committee."

"That is anarchism. Anarchism does not file reports. Anarchism cannot attend board meetings. Anarchism has no standing."

Dickens continued writing. The subcommittees were spawning sub-subcommittees. The whiteboard was running out of space. Dickens did not see this as a problem. Dickens saw this as evidence that he needed a second whiteboard.

Twain began labeling everything in the room simultaneously.

Not selectively. Not strategically. Everything. She had arrived at the conclusion that if the room was going to be renovated, the room should be documented first, and documentation, for Twain, meant labeling, and labeling meant everything, and everything meant the chairs, the table, the walls, the floor, the ceiling, the door, the doorknob, the hinges on the door, the light switch, the electrical outlet next to the light switch, the baseboard beneath the electrical outlet, and the small crack in the baseboard that had been there since before the Club existed and which Twain labeled: ORIGINAL (PRE-INSTITUTIONAL).

She labeled the fire extinguisher. The label read: DO NOT LABEL. This was not a contradiction. This was Twain's way of identifying things that should be left alone, and the identification of things that should be left alone required a label because, without the label how would anyone know the thing should be left alone, and this logic was circular and Twain knew it was circular and she did not care because circularity was not a flaw in a labeling system.

Circularity was proof that the system was comprehensive enough to include itself.

Melville's ice melted.

This was the event that elevated the situation from manageable to critical. Melville's ice had been in the cooler since the morning. The cooler was rated for six hours. The meeting was in its fourth hour, which was longer than any meeting in the Club's history, because the combination of Parker's ideas and Dickens's committees and Twain's labeling and Austen's standing up had extended the proceedings past the point where normal meetings ended and into the territory where meetings become events and events become crises and crises become the things that clubs remember for the rest of their existence.

The ice had been sitting in the cooler for longer than usual because Melville had opened the cooler seventeen times during the meeting, once each time he needed reassurance, and each opening let warm air in, and the warm air was the enemy, and the enemy was cumulative, and the cumulation was silent, and the silence was how the ice was lost.

Melville opened the cooler for the eighteenth time and found water.

Not ice. Not slush. Not the transitional state between solid and liquid that Melville called "compromise ice" and considered a personal failure. Water. Clear, still, room temperature water that had once been ice and was now the memory of ice, the ghost of ice, the evidence that ice had been here and was gone, and the going was irreversible, and irreversibility was the thing that Melville could not accept about any situation but especially about ice.

"The ice," Melville said.

He said it the way a man says the name of something

he has lost and is not yet able to process the losing. He said it the way a sentence begins when the sentence does not know how to end, because the ending is too large for the grammar.

"The ice is gone."

He held the cooler. He held it the way you hold a thing that has failed you, not with anger but with the bewildered tenderness of a person who trusted a container and the container did not hold. The cooler had one job. The cooler's job was to keep the ice ice. The cooler had not kept the ice, ice. The cooler had kept the ice for a while and then the while had ended and the ice had ended with it, and Melville was standing in a room full of people who were arguing about committees and labels and renovation and social media, and none of them had noticed that the ice was gone, and the not noticing was the thing that broke him, because the ice was the most important thing in the room and the room had not even noticed its death.

"The ice is the primary issue," Melville said, louder now, loud enough that Dickens stopped writing and Twain stopped labeling and Austen looked up from the minutes and the Psychoanalyst looked away from Parker, whom he had been analyzing since Parker arrived and about whom he had already formed seventeen conclusions, none of which he had been asked for and all of which he intended to share at the first available opportunity.

"The ice is the primary issue, and it has always been the primary issue, and while you have been arguing about committees and labels and paint colors and branding, the ice has melted. The ice has melted because this meeting has lasted too long. The meeting has lasted too long because it is about things that should not require a meeting. We should not need a meeting to decide whether to keep our own chairs. We should not need a committee to protect a pineapple. We should not need labels on the baseboards. We need ice. We need cold, correct, properly compressed nugget ice, and the ice is gone, and it is gone because we spent four hours discussing the architecture of a building that was not on fire until people arrived with blueprints."

The room was quiet.

Then Woolf unplugged her light.

Woolf's fluorescent work light had been plugged in during the inspection and had remained plugged in during the board meeting because Woolf had not been near the outlet during either event. But now Woolf walked to the wall, crouched beside the outlet, and pulled the plug. The fluorescent light died. The room dimmed. The dimming was immediate and profound, not because the room was dark but because the room had been lit by two kinds of light, the natural light from the window and Woolf's artificial light from the wall, and the removal of the artificial light did not make the room darker. It made the room more itself.

The snack table, which had been bleached into forensic visibility by the fluorescent light for weeks, settled back into the soft, forgiving illumination of the afternoon. The crackers looked like crackers again, not like evidence. The cheese looked like cheese. The mixed nuts looked like a reasonable choice made by a reasonable person, not like a still life arranged for documentation.

"The light was wrong," Woolf said. She said it simply. She said it as if she were reporting a fact she had only just confirmed, though the fact had been visible since the first meeting, and the confirmation had been available since the inspection; it was not new information but newly accepted information, which is a different thing.

"The light was wrong because I brought it. I brought it to see better. I brought it because I believed that seeing better was the same as seeing correctly, and it is not. Seeing better is seeing more. Seeing correctly is seeing what is there. The fluorescent light showed us more of the snacks and less of the room. The light was a version of what Shelley had done. What the Department has done. What the brochure, the survey, the grant, the board, and the programming have done. They have all added light. They have all made things more visible. And the visibility has made things less true."

She looked at the unplugged light leaning against the wall.

"I should have unplugged it sooner," she said.

Then Byron knocked the pineapple off the table.

He did not knock it deliberately. Byron never did anything deliberately. Byron operated on the principle that all surfaces were his, and that all objects on those surfaces were subject to his gravitational field, and his gravitational field was chaotic, and chaos does not deliberate. He was chasing a puzzle piece that Dickens had placed too close to the edge of the table while sketching his subcommittee structure. The puzzle piece fell. Byron lunged. His small body, which operated at a scale it did not recognize, collided with the pineapple, and the pineapple, for the first time in the history of the Evergreen Club, left the table.

The pineapple fell.

It fell the way all important things fall, slowly enough that everyone could see it happening and no one could stop it. It fell with the heavy, turning descent of an object that has been in one place for so long that the falling itself seems impossible, the way a mountain seems impossible to move until it moves, and then the impossibility is replaced by the much larger impossibility of the mountain being somewhere it has never been.

The pineapple hit the floor.

It did not break. Pineapples are not fragile. Pineapples are built the way pineapples are built, with an exterior that is armored, an interior that is dense, and a crown that is sharp enough to discourage anything that is not committed. The pineapple hit the floor and rolled, once, twice, three times, and came to rest under the chair next to mine, the empty chair, the chair that nobody sat in, the chair that Poe had chosen during the inspection as his observation post.

The room froze.

The pineapple was not on the table. The pineapple had been on the table since the Club's founding. The pineapple on the table was not a decoration, a symbol, a mascot, or a brand element. The pineapple on the table was the Club. The pineapple not on the table was a room that had lost its center, and a room that has lost its center is a room that does not know what it is, and not knowing what you are is the thing that lets other people tell you.

Byron sat on the edge of the table where the pineapple had been. He sat in the absence with the oblivious satisfaction of a creature who has caused a catastrophe and does not recognize it as a catastrophe because catastrophe is a human category, and Byron does not participate in human categories. Byron participates in Byron categories, and Byron's categories include: things I have sat on, things I have knocked over, things I have bitten, and things I have not yet encountered, and the categories do not include consequences because consequences require memory and memory requires regret and regret requires the understanding that your actions affect others, and Byron did not have this understanding and would never have this under standing and this was the quality that made Byron both the most destructive and the most free creature in the room.

Hemingway, who had been standing by the door for the entire meeting, walked to the empty chair. He walked with purpose. He walked with the deliberate, straight line gait of a dog who has identified a thing that needs to be done and is going to do it without committee approval, without a subcommittee, without a label, and without a survey asking whether the doing should be done.

He crouched. He reached under the chair. His mouth, which was large enough and gentle enough to carry things without damaging them, closed around the pineapple. He picked it up. He carried it across the room, his head held high, the pineapple balanced in his jaws with the care of a creature carrying something that matters, and he placed it back on the table.

The pineapple was slightly damp. The pineapple was slightly dented on one side, with a small depression where the floor had pressed against the skin. The crown was tilted. The posture was no longer regal. The pineapple looked like it had been through something.

The pineapple looked like the rest of us.

Steinbeck, who had been lying on the floor through the entire incident, looked at Hemingway. Steinbeck wagged his tail. The tail wag was not a congratulations. It was recognition. Steinbeck recognized what Hemingway had done the way one old worker recognizes another old worker completing a task that needed doing, not with celebration but with the quiet acknowledgment that the work was done and the doing was enough.

Austen straightened the pineapple. He straightened it the way he always straightened it, with the small, precise adjustment of a man who maintains things because maintaining things is how he says the things he does not say with words. The pineapple was back. The pineapple was dented. The pineapple was wet. The pineapple was not what it had been before it fell, because nothing is what it was before it falls, and the falling changes the thing even when the thing survives the fall, and surviving the fall is not the same as being undamaged, but it is enough, and enough was the Club's standard.

The room was quiet.

The quiet was different from the other quiets. The other quiets had been the silence of assessment, or the silence of resistance, or the silence of people waiting for someone else to speak first. This quiet was the silence of people who have seen something happen and are not yet sure what it means, but know that it means something, and that the meaning will arrive when the meaning is ready, and the meaning is not in a hurry.

The egg timer rang.

Nobody had reset it. Nobody had been watching it. The timer had been ticking through the entire crisis, counting its interval, and the interval had ended, and the ring was the ring it always was, the ring that measured nothing and meant everything, and the ring landed in the silent room like a bell in a church where the congregation had forgotten it was there.

Nobody reset it.

For a long time, nobody reset it.

Then Austen reached over and reset it. He reset it slowly. He reset it with the deliberate care of a man performing a ritual that, in this moment, has become more than a ritual. The resetting was a restoration. The resetting was a declaration. The resetting said: we are still here. The timer still rings. The room still nods. The pineapple is still on the table. We have been through something. We have survived it. We continue.

Parker sat in the corner, very quiet, holding the folder of ideas that had not been discussed since Austen stood up. The folder was closed. The sample posts were inside. The social media plan was inside. The mentorship program was inside. The renovation proposal was inside. Everything Parker had brought was inside, and inside was where it would stay, not because Parker had been defeated but because Parker had witnessed something the folder could not contain and the ideas could not address: a room that knew what it was and would not be told otherwise.

Parker looked at the pineapple. The dented, damp, slightly tilted pineapple. The pineapple that had fallen and been carried back by a dog who did not need a committee to tell him the pineapple belonged on the table.

Parker did not write anything down.

This was the first time Parker had been in the room without writing something down, and the not-writing was the beginning of something, or the end of something, or both, and the distinction between beginnings and endings is the distinction that the Evergreen Club had been trying to explain since the first letter arrived, which is that they are the same thing, and the same thing does not require a brochure.

The Psychoanalyst opened his mouth. The room looked at him. Hemingway walked to the Psychoanalyst's chair and sat on his foot.

The Psychoanalyst closed his mouth.

The room was grateful. The room expressed its gratitude by not expressing it, which is the Club's preferred method of expressing everything.

· · ·

PRIVATE LEDGER ENTRY:

Pineapple hit the floor. Hemingway carried it back. I felt the dent in my own ribs before I saw it on the fruit. Byron slept through his own crime. I wrote the Statement of Purpose and deleted every version that told the truth. The dogs are the only honest editors left. They approve by sleeping on it.

Chapter 10

THE SPEECH

The request came by email, which is the medium institutions use when they want to create a record of a thing they are about to require you to do while preserving the appearance that they are asking. An email is a letter that arrives instantly and sits permanently, and can be forwarded to people you have never met who will read it without context and form opinions about you based on sentences you wrote at nine in the morning before your coffee had taken effect. An email is a document pretending to be a conversation. The pretense is the danger.

The email was from Shelley. The email was addressed to me. The email said:

"Hi Coyote, Hope you're doing well! As we move forward with the grant application, the review committee has requested a Statement of Purpose from the Evergreen Club. This brief document (1-2 pages) articulates the Club's mission, values, and vision for the future. As the Club's resident writer, I thought you'd be the perfect person to draft this. The committee will review the statement as part of its final determination. Could you have something ready by next Thursday? Let me know if you have any questions! Best, Shelley"

The email contained two exclamation points, one "Hope you're doing well," one "perfect person," and the phrase "mission, values, and vision for the future," which is a phrase that exists in every institutional lexicon the way load bearing walls exist in buildings, not because anyone remembers who put them there but because removing them would cause the structure to collapse and the people who work inside the structure prefer the structure to stand even if nobody can remember what it was built for.

I read the email at my desk. Steinbeck was at my feet. Hemingway was by the door. The desk held the accumulating archive of the Club's contact with the Department: the four-sentence letter, the brochure with Twain's labels, my copy of the survey with its sevens, and the governance framework with the cat's paw prints on page five. The archive was growing the way archives grow, not because the past is expanding but because the present keeps becoming the past, and each new document joins the others, and the others make room because archives are generous with space and indifferent to sequence.

A Statement of Purpose. One to two pages. Articulating the Club's mission, values, and vision for the future.

The Club did not have a mission. The Club had a pineapple.

The Club did not have values. The Club had agreements, and the agreements were not written, not voted on, and not articulated, because articulating an agreement changes the agreement the way photographing a wild animal changes the animal. The animal was doing something before the photograph was taken. After the photograph, the animal is posing. The difference is invisible in the photograph and total in the animal.

The Club did not have a vision for the future. The Club had next Thursday. Next Thursday, the timer would ring and Austen would reset it, and the pineapple would preside, and the ice would be good, and the puzzle would advance by three to seven pieces and Twain would label something and Dickens would propose a committee and the Psychoanalyst would analyze someone who had not requested analysis and Byron would knock something over and Poe would not speak. That was the vision. The vision was repetition. The vision was the same thing happening again, not because the same thing was exciting, but because the same thing was real, and real things do not need a vision. Real things need a room.

I sat at the desk for a long time.

Writing is not hard. Writing is what I do. Writing is the thing that the room identified as my talent and assigned to me, the way Melville was assigned ice, and Twain was assigned labels, and Dickens was assigned the compulsive creation of organizational structures. Writing is my ice. I carry it to every room. I carry it because the room needs it, or because I need the room to need it, and the distinction between those two things is the distinction between vocation and habit, and after enough years, the distinction dissolves, and what remains is the carrying.

But this writing was different. This writing was not a letter, a response, or a draft. This writing was a statement, and a statement is a different animal from a sentence. A sentence says what you mean. A statement says what you are. And what the Club was could not be stated because stating it would fix it in place, and the Club was not fixed. The Club was alive. It moved. It shifted. It absorbed new crises and old ice and rogue cats and institutional threats and egg timer intervals that measured nothing, and the absorbing was the thing, the living, breathing absorbing that could not be captured in one to two pages of mission, values, and vision without killing the thing the pages described.

I wrote a mission statement. It took four minutes. It said:

"The Evergreen Club provides a welcoming community space where older adults engage in enriching activities that promote wellness, creativity, and social connection."

I read it. It was competent. It was professional. It was the kind of sentence that grant committees read, approve, file, and never think about again because it was designed to be approved, not to be true. The sentence could have described any organization in the Department's portfolio. The sentence could have been generated by typing "community organization mission statement" into a search engine and selecting the second result, because the first result would be too specific, the third result would be too vague, and the second result would be exactly the kind of adequate that institutional language aspires to.

I deleted it.

I wrote another one. This one said:

"The Evergreen Club is an independent gathering of older adults who meet weekly to share space, conversation, and the experience of continuing to exist in a world that has largely stopped designing things for them."

I read it. It was better. It was closer. But it was still not right because it was still explaining, and explaining the Club was the thing I had been asked to prevent. Explaining the Club was the pineapple becoming policy. Every sentence I wrote that described the Club accurately was a sentence that brought the Club closer to the thing the Department wanted it to be, which was a described thing, a defined thing, a thing with edges that could be measured, and a center that could be named.

I deleted it.

I sat at the desk. Steinbeck shifted at my feet. Hemingway remained by the door. The room was quiet in the way my room at home was always quiet, which was the quiet of a room where a person is supposed to be working and is instead sitting in the chair staring at a screen that contains nothing, and the nothing on the screen is the same nothing that the Club was made of, and writing about nothing is the hardest kind of writing because nothing is the thing that disappears when you describe it.

I went to the Club.

I did not go on a meeting day. I went on a Tuesday, which was the day the Club was empty, the day the room existed without its members, the day the chairs sat in their positions without the people who had positioned them, the day the pineapple presided over a table that held no ice and no puzzle and no labels and no cat.

Austen was there. Austen was always there. Whether Austen lived at the Club or merely arrived before anyone else and left after everyone else was a question nobody had asked because the asking would have required Austen to describe a life outside the Club, and Austen's life outside the Club was his own, and the Club's respect for what was someone's own was one of its unwritten agreements, and the agreement was maintained by the not asking.

"You are here on a Tuesday," Austen said.

"I need to sit with the pineapple."

Austen nodded as if this were the most reasonable

sentence anyone had said to him in weeks, which it probably was.

He left me alone in the room. He did not leave the
building. He left the room. The distinction was Austen's
way of providing solitude without providing absence. He
was nearby. He was available. He was not watching.

I sat in my chair. The chair that had been through
things. The chair received me the way it always received
me, with the patience of a structure that had held my
weight many times and would hold it many more times,
and did not require gratitude for the holding because the
holding was what it was for.

The pineapple was on the table. The dent from its fall
was still visible, a small impression on one side that caught
the light differently from the rest of the skin. The crown
was still slightly tilted. The pineapple had been through
something, and the something was visible, and the visibility
did not diminish the pineapple. The visibility was the
pineapple's new quality, the quality of a thing that has
fallen and returned, and the return was not the same as
never having fallen, and not being the same was not worse.
It was fuller.

I looked at the pineapple for a long time.

Then I wrote.

I did not write a mission statement. I did not write a
statement of values. I did not write a vision for the future. I
wrote a thing that was none of those things and might have
been all of them and was, in the end, just a description of
what happened in a room when the room was allowed to be
what it was.

I wrote:

"The Evergreen Club is a room.

"The room contains a pineapple that has never been

explained. It contains an egg timer that measures no known interval. It contains chairs that have been sat in by the same people for long enough that the chairs have learned the people and the people have learned the chairs. It contains a puzzle that will not be finished. It contains labels on things that did not ask to be labeled, ice that was carried from a place where the ice is correct, and a fluorescent light that has been unplugged.

"The room contains a man who opens the door before you knock and resets the timer without checking the dial and maintains the room the way a person maintains a promise, which is by showing up and doing the thing and not explaining why the thing matters, because the explaining would take longer than the doing and would be less accurate.

"The room contains a woman who moves things half an inch and then stares at the space the moving created as if the space is the point and the thing is just the tool that made the space.

"The room contains a man who starts projects that involve everyone's surface area and cannot be stopped and should not be stopped because the starting is how he says he is still here and still here is the most important thing anyone in this room can say.

"The room contains a woman who labels everything because the labeling is how she knows the world has been observed, and the observation is how she knows the world is real and reality is the thing she will not leave to chance.

"The room contains a man who carries ice because the ice is correct and correctness is the last stand of a person who has watched the world accept one compromise after another and has decided that this one thing, this one small cold thing, will not be compromised. Not on his watch. Not in his cooler. Not ever.

"The room contains a man who looks at you for three seconds and tells you who you are, and he is almost right, which is the most tiring kind of wrong, but the room tolerates him because the room tolerates everything that is sincere, and he is sincere, and his sincerity is the one thing about him that his analysis cannot reach.

"The room contains a cat who is young and breaks things and does not know he is young and does not know things break and will learn both of these facts eventually, and the room will be here when he does.

"The room contains a raven who has not spoken. The raven watches. The raven waits. The raven knows something the room does not, or the raven knows the same thing the room knows and is simply waiting for the room to know it out loud.

"The room contains two dogs. One trusts everything. One trusts nothing but stays anyway. Between them, they cover the full range of what loyalty looks like, and both versions are correct.

"The room does not have a mission. The room has a pineapple. The pineapple does not welcome. The pineapple presides. Presiding is what you do when you have been in a place long enough that your presence is the authority, and the authority does not need to be granted because it was never taken. It was simply maintained, the way a person maintains breathing, not as an achievement but as a continuation.

"The room does not have a vision for the future. The room has next Thursday. Next Thursday, the timer will ring, and someone will reset it, and someone will bring ice and someone will label something and someone will start a project and someone will stare out a window and see something no one else sees and the room will hold all of it the way rooms hold everything, which is silently and without credit and without a quarterly report.

"The room is not vibrant. The room is adequate. Adequate means enough. Enough means the room works. The room works because the people in it have agreed, without paperwork, without votes, without a board of directors, to be in the room, to let the room be what it is, and not to ask the room to be anything else.

"This is the purpose. The purpose is the room. The room is the purpose. They are the same thing, and they cannot be separated, and they cannot be put in a brochure, and they cannot be measured by a survey, and they cannot be governed by a board, and they cannot be funded by a grant without becoming something other than what they are.

"What they are is enough."

I put the pen down. The pen was a pen. The pen had done what pens do. The words were on paper. The paper was on the table next to the pineapple, and the pineapple and the paper sat side by side, the explained and the unexplained, and the explained was not better than the unexplained. The explanation was just the sound the unexplained made when it was finally asked to speak.

I brought it to the next meeting.

I read it aloud. I read it the way I had written it, which was plainly, without performance, without the inflections that writers use when they want the audience to feel something specific. I did not want the room to feel something specific. I wanted the room to hear what it already knew, said in words it had not chosen, and decide for itself whether the words were close enough.

The room was quiet.

Woolf was the first to respond. She did not speak. Something moved across her face that was not tears because Woolf did not cry in public and would not have called it crying in private and would have said, if asked, that the face does things the mind does not authorize and the authorization is not required because the face knows what the mind will not admit. Something moved across her face, and she turned to the window, and the window received whatever it was and held it in the light, and the light did not judge it.

Dickens was the second to respond. "This could be expanded," he said. "A pamphlet. A series of pamphlets. We could develop each section into a chapter. I can have a table of contents drafted by Friday."

"No," I said.

"A small pamphlet."

"No."

"An annotated version with footnotes."

"No, Dickens."

He sat back. He sat back with the acceptance of a man who has offered expansion and been denied and understands the denial even as he disagrees with it, because Dickens believed everything could be improved by being longer, and the belief was so deeply held that contradicting it required no defense. The contradiction was simply the other way of being, and Dickens could see it without adopting it, the way a person can see a mountain without climbing it.

Twain reached for her label maker. She printed one label. She placed it on the bottom of the last page.

FINAL.

The label was the smallest label Twain had ever

produced. It was one word. One word was not Twain's style. Twain's style was comprehensive, exhaustive, and multilayered. One word from Twain was the equivalent of a standing ovation from a person who does not stand and does not ovate. FINAL. The word said, " This is done." The doneness is not a suggestion. The doneness is a label. The doneness is permanent. The doneness is Twain's professional opinion, and Twain's professional opinion, once labeled, does not change.

Melville nodded. The nod was small and contained, with the quality of a man who has heard something true and is acknowledging it without elaborating, because elaboration would take the truth somewhere it did not need to go. The statement mentioned the ice. The statement had mentioned the ice correctly. The statement had said "the ice is correct," and the correctness of the statement about the correctness of the ice was, for Melville, the highest form of recognition he had ever received, and the recognition was enough, and enough was the word, and the word had been written, and the ice was in it.

Austen did not speak. Austen sat in his chair with the stillness of a man who has heard something he has been waiting to hear and is processing the hearing the way he processed everything, internally, privately, with the precision of a ledger being updated by a person who will never show the ledger to anyone because the ledger is not for display. The ledger is for accuracy. And the accuracy is for the room.

He picked up the statement. He placed it on the table next to the pineapple. He aligned it with the edge of the table. The alignment was his response.

The Psychoanalyst opened his mouth.

Hemingway sat on his foot.

The Psychoanalyst closed his mouth. Then he opened it again, because the Psychoanalyst could not be stopped by a dog on his foot any more than a river can be stopped by a stone. The river goes around the stone. The Psychoanalyst went around the dog.

"The statement," he said, "is a defense mechanism."

"The statement," I said, "is a statement."

"It describes the Club as sufficient. Sufficiency is the language of a person who has decided that asking for more is dangerous. The statement protects the Club by defining its scope as complete, which prevents external evaluation because you cannot evaluate a thing that has declared itself finished."

"The Club has not declared itself finished. The Club has declared itself enough. Finished and enough are not the same thing. Finished means nothing more will happen. Enough means what is happening is sufficient. The difference is the difference between a clock that has stopped and a clock that is keeping the time it was built to keep."

"And what time was the Club built to keep?"

"The time between egg timer rings. Which is all the time there is."

The Psychoanalyst nodded. The nod was the nod of a man who has been answered and knows the answer is good and cannot admit the answer is good because admitting the answer is good would mean his question was answered, and answered questions are closed questions, and closed questions are the end of the Psychoanalyst's usefulness, and the end of usefulness is the thing the Psychoanalyst fears more than anything, which is the thing he would diagnose in anyone else and cannot see in himself, and the not seeing is the thing that makes him almost right about everything and completely wrong about himself.

The statement sat on the table. The statement sat next to the pineapple. The pineapple did not read it. The pineapple did not need to read it. The pineapple was in it, and being in a thing you do not need to read is the definition of being understood.

The egg timer rang.

Austen reset it.

The room nodded.

The interval began.

Chapter 11

THE DECISION

The vote was held on a Thursday because Thursday was now board meeting day, and board meeting day was the day the Club conducted the business it had never asked to conduct in the format it had never asked to adopt using the language it had never asked to speak. Thursday was the day the Club put on the costume of an organization and walked through the motions of governance, and then took the costume off and went home and sat in rooms where the costume did not fit and the motions did not apply, and the language returned to the language of people who had not needed a board to know what they were.

The question before the board was whether to accept the grant.

Shelley had submitted my statement to the review committee. The review committee had reviewed it. The review committee's response was three paragraphs long and included the phrases "compelling narrative," "unique organizational culture," and "while we appreciate the creative approach, we would also need a more traditional statement of purpose for our records." The review committee had liked the statement the way a museum likes a painting, with admiration and the immediate impulse to put a frame around it and a placard beside it and a rope in front of it so that no one could touch the thing they admired, because admiration and control are, in institutional settings, the same gesture performed with different hands.

Shelley had written the traditional statement of purpose herself. She had written it using my statement as a "reference document," which is the institutional term for a thing you read before writing the thing you were going to write anyway. Her traditional statement of purpose said all the things traditional statements of purpose say. It mentioned community. It mentioned enrichment. It mentioned vibrant. It mentioned the pineapple once, parenthetically, as "a longstanding club tradition symbolizing hospitality and welcome." The parenthetical was a cage. The pineapple had been placed inside it the way a bird is placed inside a cage, with the understanding that the bird is still a bird and the cage is for the bird's protection, and the bird does not agree, but the bird cannot say so because the cage is where the bird now lives.

I did not object to Shelley's statement. Objecting to Shelley's statement would have required offering an alternative that the review committee would accept, and the only alternative the review committee would accept was a statement that sounded like Shelley's statement, which meant the only way to replace Shelley's statement was with another version of Shelley's statement, which meant the language had already been decided and the only remaining question was who would speak it, and who would speak it did not change what was said.

This is how institutions win. They do not win by force.

They win by vocabulary. They establish the words that are acceptable and the words that are not, and once the words are established, the conversation can only go where the words allow, and the words allow everything except the truth, because the truth does not use the words. The truth uses different words, words like "adequate" and "enough" and "pineapple," and those words are not in the institutional vocabulary, and words that are not in the vocabulary do not appear in the record, and things that do not appear in the record do not exist, and things that do not exist cannot be funded.

The vote was simple. The board had five members. Chair: Shelley. Vice Chair: Dickens. Secretary: Austen. Treasurer: Melville. At-Large Member: a young woman named Harper from the Department's volunteer pool, not the wellness Harper but a different Harper, a second Harper, which the Department produced with the reliable consistency of an institution that has a limited number of names and distributes them without checking whether the name is already in use in the same room. The second Harper was twenty-four, had a degree in public administration, and had been told that she was representing "the youth perspective," which is a phrase that means a young person has been placed in a room and asked to be young in it, and the youngness is the contribution, and the contribution is the presence, and the presence is the representation, and the representation is the check mark on the form that says intergenerational engagement has been achieved.

The second Harper had attended two meetings. She had been quiet at both. She had watched the room the way a person watches a film in a language they do not speak, following the action without understanding the dialogue, inferring meaning from gesture and tone and the particular way that Austen reset the egg timer, which communicated more than any sentence Harper had heard in her twenty-four years of sentences, though she did not know what it communicated and would not know for another thirty or forty years, and by then the knowing would be the kind of knowing that cannot be explained to someone who has not waited thirty or forty years, which is the kind of knowing the Club was built to hold.

Byron had been officially denied the At-Large seat. The denial was recorded in the minutes. The minutes said: "Motion to seat Byron (cat, age 3) as At-Large Member denied by Chair on jurisdictional grounds. Cat present at meeting. Cat sat on denial."

The non-board members were present for the vote because the Evergreen Club did not distinguish between board meetings and regular meetings in any meaningful way. The board meeting was a regular meeting with an agenda stapled to it, and the agenda was Shelley's and the staple was metaphorical and the meeting was the same meeting it had always been except that at some point during the meeting Shelley would call the board to order and the board would pretend to be in order and the pretending would last long enough to conduct business and then the pretending would stop and the meeting would resume being a meeting.

"I'd like to call the board to order," Shelley said.

She said it with the practiced formality of a person performing a role she believes in, and the belief was genuine, and the genuineness was the thing that made the formality bearable, because formal proceedings led by a cynic are oppressive, and formal proceedings led by a believer are merely strange, and the Club could tolerate strange. The Club was strange. Strange was the Club's medium, the way water is a fish's medium, and you do not object to water when you are a fish. You swim.

"The matter before the board," Shelley said, "is the acceptance of the Community Enrichment Partnership Grant, in the amount of forty-eight thousand dollars over two years, subject to the terms and conditions outlined in the grant agreement."

She placed the grant agreement on the table. It was the same thirty-two pages it had been when it arrived, but it was now accompanied by a signature page and a cover letter from the Department's director, and the cover letter said that the Department was "thrilled to support the Evergreen Club's mission of community enrichment," and the word "thrilled" was doing the same work in the cover letter that "vibrant" was doing in the brochure, which was the work of pretending that the institution had feelings about the transaction when the institution had only policies, and the policies were the feelings, and the feelings were the policies, and neither one had ever been thrilled about anything.

"Discussion," Shelley said.

Austen spoke first. Austen always spoke first in matters of governance because governance was his jurisdiction, the way the ice was Melville's, and the labels were Twain's, and the committees were Dickens's. He spoke from the Secretary's position, which was the position Shelley had assigned him and which he had accepted and which he had converted, through the sheer force of his presence, from a clerical role into something closer to what he had always been, which was the conscience of the room.

"The grant," Austen said, "provides forty-eight thousand dollars. The grant requires a board of directors, which we now have. The grant requires quarterly reports, which I will write. The grant requires programming, which has been implemented. The grant requires a statement of purpose, which has been submitted. The grant requires everything the Department has asked for, and the Department has received everything it has asked for. The question is not whether we can accept the grant. We can. The question is whether accepting the grant changes what we are."

He paused. The pause was Austen's primary rhetorical instrument, the silence into which the room placed its own understanding.

"I believe it does," he said. "I believe it already has. I believe the board changed us. I believe the programming changed us. I believe the brochure changed us. I believe the survey changed us. I believe each step was small, and each step was reasonable, and each step moved us closer to a version of this Club that the Department recognizes, because the Department designed it. And the version the Department designed is not the version we built. The version we built has a pineapple that does not explain itself and a timer that measures nothing and chairs that know their people and ice that is carried in by hand because the correct ice does not come from a machine that answers to a budget committee."

He looked at the grant agreement.

"The money will help," he said. "The money will pay for a coordinator we do not need, programming we did not request, and facility improvements we have not asked for. The money will pay for the Scotsman SCN60."

He looked at Melville.

"The money will buy the machine. And the machine will make the ice. And the ice will be here, in this room, on demand, and it will be good ice, and it will be correct ice, and it will be ice that Melville does not have to carry, and Melville not having to carry the ice sounds like relief and looks like relief and on every practical measure is relief. But the carrying was never the burden. The carrying was the point. The carrying was Melville saying, every week, with his hands and his car and his time and his loyalty to a specific Sonic Drive-In on Fourth Street near the overpass, that this room matters enough to bring something to. And a machine does not say that. A machine says the budget committee approved a line item. A machine says the grant paid for it. A machine says the ice is provided by the institution, and institutional ice is not Melville's ice, and the difference is not about the ice."

Melville was holding his bag. The bag was full. The bag was cold. The bag was from the Sonic Drive-In on Fourth Street, the one near the overpass, not the one near the mall. The bag was the bag it had always been, the temporary vessel of a permanent commitment, and Melville held it the way he always held it, with the care of a man who understands that the thing in his hands is not the thing in his hands. The thing in his hands is the carrying.

Dickens spoke next. Dickens had prepared remarks. The remarks were seven pages long and included a historical analysis of grant-funded organizations, a comparative study of institutional capture in community settings, a flowchart depicting the decision tree for acceptance versus rejection, and an appendix containing the minutes of every subcommittee meeting Dickens had convened in the past three weeks, all of which had been attended only by Dickens because the subcommittees had only one member, which was Dickens, but the minutes were thorough and the proceedings were recorded and the record was complete even if the attendance was solitary.

"I have prepared a comprehensive analysis," Dickens said.

"Summarize," Austen said.

"The comprehensive analysis resists summarization. That is what makes it comprehensive."

"Summarize it anyway."

Dickens looked at his seven pages. He looked at them the way a parent looks at a child who has been told to stay home. The pages wanted to go out. The pages had things to say. The pages had been prepared and organized, and annotated, and they deserved their moment.

"The summary," Dickens said, with the visible pain of a man compressing something that was designed to expand, "is that the grant will create more structure than we can dismantle. The structure will produce requirements. The requirements will produce documentation. The documentation will produce a version of this Club that exists on paper and the paper version will eventually replace the room version because paper outlasts rooms and departments outlast clubs and the only things that survive institutions are the things institutions cannot describe, and the grant is the Department's attempt to describe us, and the description will be permanent, and permanence is how they win."

He set down the seven pages. The seven pages sat on the table, looking truncated and disappointed, like a novel reduced to a dust jacket.

"But," Dickens said, and the "but" was the hinge, the turn, the moment where Dickens's analysis departed from his conclusion the way a river departs from the direction the map predicted, "I also believe that we have already changed. The board exists. The programming exists. The brochure exists. The survey exists. We cannot unexist these things. We can only decide whether we control the next step or whether the Department controls the next step, and controlling the next step requires resources, and resources require the grant, and the grant requires the things we have already given."

The room heard this. The room heard the loop. The loop was the trap. The trap was not Shelley's trap and not the Department's trap. The trap was the trap that every institution sets without setting it, the trap that works by making each step logical and each logical step a step closer to the next logical step and the next logical step a step closer to the step after that, and by the time you see the destination, the steps have been walked and the walking cannot be unwound.

Twain did not speak. Twain labeled. She produced three labels and placed them on the table.

The first label read: ACCEPT. The second label read: DECLINE. The third label read: BOTH WRONG.

The third label was the most honest thing in the room. Both options were wrong. Accepting the grant meant becoming the Department's version of the Club. Declining the grant meant the Department would continue its campaign without the Club's participation, which meant the Club would be described without its consent, which was worse than being described with its consent, which was already bad. The choice was between two kinds of losing, and the only honest label for two kinds of losing was both wrong, and Twain had labeled it, and the labeling was the closest anyone in the room came to solving the problem, which was not a solution but at least an accurate description of the absence of a solution.

Woolf spoke from the window. She spoke to the light, or to the curtain, or to the space between the light and the curtain, which was the space where Woolf's thoughts lived, the space between what was visible and what was true.

"The room will survive the grant, the way it survived the brochure and the survey and the board and the programming and the inspection," she said. "The room will survive because the room is not the structure. The room is the people. The people are not the organization. The people are the agreements. The agreements are not the documents. The agreements are the silence between the documents, the things we decided without deciding, the things we know without saying. The grant can fund the structure. The grant cannot fund the silence. The silence is ours. The silence has always been ours. And as long as the silence is ours, the room is ours, and the room is the Club, and the Club is the pineapple, and the pineapple does not answer to a grant committee."

Melville spoke. He spoke, holding the bag. He spoke the way he always spoke about important things, which was directly and about ice.

"I vote against the grant," he said.

He said it clearly, without the elaboration that usually accompanied his positions on ice-related matters, which was every matter. He said it the way a man says a thing he has decided, and the decision is final and the finality is not anger but resolution, the resolution of a man who has weighed the Scotsman SCN60 against the bag in his hands and has chosen the bag.

"The machine would make the ice," he said. "The machine would make the ice here, in this room, every day. The machine would make sixty pounds of nugget ice at the correct compression ratio. The machine would end the drive. The machine would end the carrying. The machine would end the worry about condensation and cooler failure, and the one time the Sonic on Fourth Street was closed for renovation, and I had to drive to the one near the mall, and the ice was wrong, and I brought it anyway because wrong ice is better than no ice, but not by much."

He looked at the bag.

"But the ice from the machine would not be my ice. My ice is the ice I chose. My ice is the ice I carried. My ice is the ice from a specific place on a specific street brought to a specific room by a specific person who decided, years ago, that this room deserved the correct ice and that he would be the one to bring it. The machine does not decide. The machine produces. Production is not devotion. Production is a budget line. Devotion is a man in a car with a bag of ice driving across town because the room matters and the ice matters and the carrying is how you say both of those things without saying either of them."

He set the bag on the table, next to the pineapple, in the spot it had occupied since the first meeting, the spot that was not assigned and not labeled and not documented but was Melville's spot for Melville's ice, and the spot would remain Melville's spot as long as Melville carried the ice, and Melville would carry the ice as long as the room was the room, and the room would be the room as long as the pineapple presided, and the pineapple would preside as long as nobody explained it.

"The bag stays," Melville said.

The Psychoanalyst voted for the grant. He voted for it with the confidence of a man who has analyzed the situation and arrived at the conclusion that the analysis supports, which was the conclusion the analysis was always going to support, because the Psychoanalyst's analysis always supported the position that required more analysis, and the grant would produce an organization that required more analysis, and more analysis was the Psychoanalyst's natural habitat.

"The Club's resistance to the grant is a manifestation of its fear of external validation," he said. "The grant offers legitimacy, and the refusal of legitimacy is the refusal to be seen, and the refusal to be seen is the defense of a self that has not yet been fully examined."

"The self has been fully examined," I said. "It has been examined by you, at every meeting, without invitation, for months. It has been examined to the point where the examination is the thing that needs examining."

"And there it is," he said. "The recursive deflection. You use critique of the process to avoid engaging with the content."

"I use critique of the process because the process is critiquing me, and the least I can do is return the favor."

Hemingway sat on his foot. The Psychoanalyst continued talking. Hemingway continued sitting. The equilibrium held.

The second Harper voted for the grant because the second Harper had been sent by the Department and the Department expected a vote for the grant and the second Harper was twenty-four and had been in the room for two meetings and did not yet understand that the egg timer measured nothing and the pineapple was not a symbol and the ice was not just ice, and understanding these things required time, and time was the thing the vote was about, and the vote was happening now, and now was too soon for the second Harper to know what she was voting on.

She voted for the grant politely, quietly, and with the discomfort of a person who senses she is missing something but cannot identify what.

Dickens voted against the grant. He voted against it despite his seven-page analysis, which had concluded that the grant was a logical step, because Dickens's seven-page analysis was his brain's vote and his brain's vote was not the same as his vote, and his vote came from the part of him that had spent seven months working on a puzzle that was eleven percent complete and did not need funding to continue and would not be improved by a facility upgrade and could not be accelerated by a coordinator. The puzzle would be finished when the puzzle was finished. The Club would be the Club when the Club was the Club. And Dickens, for all his committees, and flowcharts and subcommittees and napkin plans, understood that the Club was not a project. The Club was a room. And you do not fund a room. You inhabit it.

Austen voted against the grant.

He voted without a speech. He voted with a single word. The word was "No."

The "No" was the smallest thing Austen had ever said in the Club and the largest thing he had ever meant. The "No" was the four-sentence letter compressed into two letters. The "No" was the governance framework rejected in a syllable. The "No" was every reset of the egg timer, every opening of the door before the knock, every straightening of the pineapple, every trained chair, and every forgiven carpet and every act of maintenance that Austen had performed since the Club's founding, all of it compressed into a word that said: this room is mine. Not mine as in ownership. Mine as in responsibility. Mine, as in I built it and I maintain it, and I will not hand the maintenance to a department that does not know the difference between maintaining a room and managing a program.

The vote was three to two against the grant.

Shelley counted the votes. She counted them carefully, with the precision of a person performing a duty she believes in, even when the outcome is not the one she expected. She wrote the result in her notebook. She wrote it clearly, legibly, in the handwriting that would become a record, and the record would be filed, and the filing would be the end of the grant application, and the end of the grant application would be the end of this particular campaign, though not the end of the Department, because departments do not end. Departments continue. That is what makes them departments.

"The vote is three to two against acceptance," Shelley said.

She said it professionally. She said it with the composure of a person who has lost a vote and will process the loss later, in private, in the way that people who believe in processes process things, which is by reviewing the steps and identifying the point where the outcome diverged from the projection and adjusting the projection for next time, because there is always a next time, and next time is where departments live.

She gathered her documents. She placed them in the portfolio, which was now so battered that it looked less like a portfolio and more like a survivor, a leather object that had endured months of cat punctures and survey residue and governance frameworks and grant applications and had emerged still functional and still holding together, the way all things that have been through things emerge, which is diminished and intact and carrying the marks of every encounter.

I walked Shelley to the door.

This was not a board function. This was not a governance function. This was the function of a person walking another person to a door, because the walk is the space where things that could not be said in the meeting can be said outside, and the outside is where the truth lives when the inside is full of process.

"You did good work," I said.

"The vote went the other way," she said.

"The vote went the way the room went. The room was always going to go this way. You could not have changed it because the thing you were trying to change is the thing the room is made of, and you cannot change what a room is made of from the outside. You can only change what it looks like, and what it looks like was never the point."

Shelley looked at me. She looked at me with the expression of a person who is hearing something she almost understands but cannot accommodate because accommodating it would mean releasing the thing she holds, and the thing she holds is the belief that helping is possible and helping looks like structure and structure looks like grants and grants look like progress and progress is the evidence that the helping worked. Releasing that belief would mean standing in a room without a structure and without a grant and without evidence and trusting that the room was enough, and trusting that the room was enough was the thing the Club had been doing since its founding, and the doing was invisible, and invisible things are the hardest things for a person with a clipboard to believe in.

"You're welcome to visit," I said. "Not as a liaison. Not as a chair. As a person. The door is open. Austen opens it before you knock."

"I might," she said.

She said "I might" the way people say "I might" when they mean "I will think about it" and "I will think about it" means "I do not know how to be in a room without a role" and not knowing how to be in a room without a role is the most common condition of people who have spent their careers inside institutions, and the condition is not a flaw. The condition is a shape. Shelley was shaped by the Department the way the rest of us were shaped by the Club, and the shapes were different, but the shaping was the same, and the shaping was just the world pressing against you until you fit the space you occupy.

She left. She walked to her car. She carried the portfolio. She carried the tote bag with Byron's claw marks and **BUILDING BRIDGES, BUILDING COMMUNITY**, and the scars of months of trying to help a room that did not want the help she was offering, not because the room did not want help, but because the help was not help. The help was replacement, and the room knew the difference even if Shelley did not, and knowing the difference was what the room was for.

She would be fine. She would find another project. She would find another room. She would carry her clipboard and her warmth and her genuine belief that the world is improved by structure into a place that wanted to be improved by structure, and the place would be grateful, and the structure would be built, and the building would be the help, and the help would be real, and it would not be here.

I went back inside.

The room was the room.

Austen was at the table. The pineapple was on the table. The egg timer was beside the pineapple. The grant agreement was on the table, unsigned, unclaimed, a document that had been voted on and denied and was now just paper, and paper without approval is just paper, and paper is what the pineapple had been sitting next to for months, and the pineapple had outlasted all of it.

Twain peeled the labels off the grant agreement. She peeled them with the slow care of a person removing bandages from a wound that has healed. The labels came off cleanly. Beneath them, the grant agreement looked like what it was, which was a proposal that had been proposed and declined, and the declining was clean, and the cleanness was the room's gift to itself, and the gift was the right to say no.

She placed one final label on the cover page.

It read: DECLINED WITH DIGNITY.

Austen reset the egg timer.

The timer rang.

The room nodded.

Private Ledger Entry:

We said no. The room got louder by getting quieter. I keep waiting for the next letter, the next Shelley, the next clipboard. Nothing arrives. Austen reset the timer as if nothing had happened. I sat in the chair that has been through things and realized the chair, and I are the same thing now: still here, still adequate, still refusing to explain why.

Chapter 12

THE RESET

The meeting after the vote was on a Thursday, but it was not a board meeting. There was no board. The board had been dissolved by the act of declining the grant, the way a puddle is dissolved by the sun, not through force but through the removal of the thing that was sustaining it, and the thing that was sustaining the board was the grant, and the grant was gone, and the board evaporated on the same schedule as the funding that had conjured it.

Shelley did not come. This was expected. The absence was not hostile, was not permanent, and was not a statement. It was the absence of a person who no longer had a reason to be in a room she had only entered because the reason existed, and the reason had been voted off the table alongside the grant agreement, and the table was now lighter for it, and the pineapple had more space, and the pineapple used the space the way it used all space, which was by presiding over it without comment.

Parker did not come. This was also expected. Parker had been sent by the Department, and the Department had recalled Parker the way a navy recalls a ship, not because the ship had failed but because the mission had ended, and a ship without a mission is a cost, and costs without missions are the first things departments eliminate, because departments understand costs the way Melville understands ice, which is personally and without negotiation.

The second Harper did not come. The second Harper had attended two meetings, voted once, and been the youngest person in a room full of people who had earned their chairs through decades of sitting in them, and the earning was not visible to someone who had not done it, and the not-doing was not Harper's fault. The not-doing was a condition of being twenty-four in a room built for people who were not twenty-four, and the condition would change when Harper was no longer twenty-four, but that would take time, and time was the thing you could not send someone to provide on your behalf.

The room was smaller. Not physically. The room was the same room it had always been, the same beige walls and forgiving carpets and trained furniture and calm lighting that Austen had built and maintained since the founding. The room was smaller in the way rooms become smaller when the people who do not belong in them leave. The room was concentrated. The room became more itself. The dilution was over. The solution was back to its original strength.

Austen opened the door before I knocked.

"The chairs have been moved," he said.

He said it the way he had said it before the inspection, but this time the tone was different. This time the tone was satisfaction. Austen had moved the chairs. Austen had moved them back from whatever intermediate positions they had drifted to during the weeks of board meetings, programming, inspections, and votes. He had moved them back to their original positions, the positions established by the gravitational field of the room, and the field was generated by the pineapple at the center and the people around it, and the distances between the people, and the distances were the Club's constitution, unwritten, unvoted, and exact.

My chair was where my chair belonged. The chair that had been through things. The chair received me with the familiar patience that I had come to rely on, the patience of a thing that exists for one purpose and performs that purpose without complaint and without credit.

Steinbeck circled twice and lay down at my feet. Hemingway walked to the door, assessed the perimeter, and took his position. The positions were correct. The room was correct. The correctness was the thing that had been missing during the weeks of formalization, the particular quality that a room has when it is arranged by the people who inhabit it rather than by the people who manage it.

Twain arrived and began removing labels.

This was unprecedented. Twain did not remove labels. Twain applied labels. Applying labels was her function, her art, and her contribution to the room's self knowledge. Removing labels was the opposite of her function, and the opposite of a person's function is either a crisis or a renewal; this was a renewal, and the renewal required removing everything that had been labeled during the occupation, because the occupation's labels were not Twain's labels. Twain's labels described the room. The Department's labels described the Department's idea of the room. And the Department's idea of the room was leaving with the Department.

She peeled the Department's labels from the programming boxes. She peeled the institutional name tags from the wall where they had been hung. She peeled the laminated schedule from the table where it had been lying face down under Byron for weeks, and Byron watched her peel it with the disinterested attention of a cat who has been sleeping on a thing and has just learned that the thing was important, and the learning does not change his opinion of the thing, which is that it was a surface and surfaces exist to be slept on.

She did not remove her own labels. Her labels stayed. The spice rack remained labeled. OREGANO (ADEQUATE). PAPRIKA (ASPIRATIONAL). CINNAMON (OVERPERFORMING). The egg timer remained TEMPORAL GOVERNANCE (AUTONOMOUS). The pineapple's forbidden label remained: MANAGEMENT (DO NOT EXPLAIN). The label maker remained ESSENTIAL PERSONNEL.

Twain's labels were the room's language. The Department's labels were a translation. The translation was being removed. The original remained.

When she was finished, she printed one new label and placed it on the wall near the door, where the laminated schedule had been posted, where Bennett's clipboard had paused, and where Shelley's brochure had been displayed.

The label read: UNDER ORIGINAL MANAGEMENT.

Dickens arrived carrying the puzzle box. He had taken the puzzle home during the final weeks of the grant campaign, which was the first time the puzzle had left the Club, and the leaving was itself a symptom of the disruption, because the puzzle belonged in the room and the room belonged to the puzzle, and removing one from the other was like removing a word from a sentence. The sentence still existed, but it no longer said what it had been saying.

He placed the box on the coffee table. He opened it. He laid out the assembled portions, which included the complete border, one confirmed corner, the barn, a section of sky that he had expanded during the exile to include what might have been a cloud or might have been a second barn or might have been the puzzle's commentary on the futility of certainty, and a new section of green that connected the maybe-tree to the maybe-other-barn in a way that suggested the pastoral landscape was more complex than anyone had anticipated.

"Twelve percent," Dickens said.

"Up from eleven," I said.

"One percent progress during a period of institutional crisis. I consider that a triumph. Most organizations lose ground during a crisis. We gained a percentage point. That is resilience measured in cardboard."

He resumed work. His fingers moved across the pieces with the familiar, practiced motion of a man who has been looking for edges his entire life and will continue looking for edges until the edges are found or the looking becomes the thing, and the looking had long ago become the thing, and Dickens knew this, and the knowing did not change the looking, because Dickens was not searching for the completed puzzle. Dickens was searching for the next piece, and the next piece was always enough.

Melville arrived with the ice.

He arrived the way he always arrived, carrying the bag with both hands, holding it against his chest, the bag from the Sonic Drive-In on Fourth Street near the over-pass, the same bag, the same ice, the same drive, the same devotion. He walked to the table and placed the bag in its spot, the spot next to the pineapple, the spot that the Scotsman SCN60 would have replaced if the grant had been accepted, the spot that remained Melville's spot because the grant had not been accepted, and the machine had not been purchased, and the ice was still carried by hand.

Melville did not mention the ice machine. He did not mention the grant. He did not mention the vote. He placed the bag in its spot, opened his cooler, and began filling glasses with the precise, ceremonial attention of a man performing a sacrament he invented and observes alone.

He filled a glass for Austen. He filled a glass for me. He filled a glass for Dickens, who took it without looking up from the puzzle. He filled a glass for Twain, who accepted it and labeled it: CORRECT.

He filled a glass for Woolf, who was by the window. Woolf took the glass and held it against the light and watched the ice catch the sun and scatter it into small, moving patterns on the wall, and the patterns were the kind of thing Woolf noticed and nobody else noticed, and the noticing was Woolf's gift to the room, and the gift was invisible, and invisible gifts are the only kind the Club traded in.

He did not fill a glass for the Psychoanalyst. This was not an oversight. Melville had made a decision about the Psychoanalyst's ice privileges during the vote, when the Psychoanalyst had voted for the grant, and the decision was that the Psychoanalyst could pour his own ice from the communal supply but would not be served personally, because personal service was a form of devotion and devotion was reserved for people who had voted to protect the bag, and the Psychoanalyst had voted for the machine.

The Psychoanalyst noticed. The Psychoanalyst noticed everything. "Interesting," he said. "The withholding of ice as a form of social discipline. The cold shoulder made literal."

"The ice is available," Melville said. "The service is not."

"And the distinction matters to you."

"The distinction is the only thing that has ever mattered to me."

The Psychoanalyst poured his own ice. He poured it without comment, which was the most restrained thing the Psychoanalyst had done since joining the Club, and the restraint was not growth. The restraint was the recognition that some distinctions cannot be analyzed without destroying them, and the Psychoanalyst had, for the first time, encountered a distinction he did not want to destroy. The distinction between being served ice and pouring your own ice was the distinction between being inside Melville's circle of devotion and being outside it, and the Psychoanalyst, who had spent his career studying the circles other people drew, had just discovered what it felt like to be outside one, and the feeling was not something he could annotate.

Woolf plugged in the fluorescent light.

The room looked at her.

She plugged it in, and the harsh brightness flooded the snack table, and the crackers became forensic, and the cheese became clinical, and the mixed nuts threw back the glare with the same defiant energy they had always thrown it back with.

Then she unplugged it.

Then she plugged it in again.

Then she unplugged it.

She stood by the outlet, holding the plug, looking at the light the way she had looked at the window and the curtain and the colors on the windowsill and every other thing she had looked at since the first meeting, which was the way you look at something when you are trying to see not the thing but the question the thing is asking.

"The light is mine," she said. "I brought it. It was wrong. But it was mine. The wrongness does not make it not mine. The wrongness makes it the wrong version of a thing I did, and the wrong version of a thing I did is still a thing I did, and taking it away completely is not the same as choosing not to use it. Taking it away says the light should never have existed. Choosing not to use it says the light existed, and I learned from it, and the learning is mine, and the light stays in the room as evidence that the room is a place where you can bring the wrong thing and the wrong thing can stay."

She placed the unplugged light in the corner, next to the wall, standing upright, neither hidden nor displayed. Present but not active. A memorial to the wrong idea that had been brought with the right intentions.

Twain labeled it: RETIRED (WITH HONORS).

The room was filling with the things that had been missing. Not things that had been removed. Things that had been displaced. The displacement was subtle, the kind of displacement that happens when a room is occupied by an idea that is not the room's idea, and the room's own ideas get pushed to the margins, the way furniture gets pushed to the walls when someone decides the center of the room should be used for something organized.

The center of the room was the pineapple again. Just the pineapple. The pineapple, the egg timer, the table, and the space around the table, where the Club's gravity held everything in its orbit. No whiteboard at the not front. No semicircle. No laminated schedule. No programming boxes.

No grant agreement. No brochure. No survey collection box. Just the room, the people, the animals, the ice, the puzzle, the labels, and the silence that the Club had built out of the agreement to be in the room without being asked to explain why being in the room was enough.

Byron climbed onto the table. He circled the pineapple once, which was fewer circles than his usual ritual, and the reduction in circles was either efficiency or maturity or the simple fact that the pineapple had been circled so many times that additional circles were redundant, and Byron, despite his youth and his chaos and his complete inability to recognize the consequences of his actions, was capable of learning that some things did not require the full treatment. He sat beside the pineapple. He placed one paw on its crown. The pineapple and the cat sat together on the table, the presider and the disruptor, the thing that never moved and the thing that never stopped moving, and the two of them together were the Club's coat of arms, if the Club had been the kind of place that had a coat of arms, which it was not, because coats of arms require a design committee and the Club did not have a design committee and never would because Dickens would volunteer to chair it and the chair would produce subcommittees and the subcommittees would produce the kind of structure that the Club had just spent months dismantling.

The egg timer rang.

Austen reset it. He reset it with the motion that was the motion, the motion that had been interrupted and redirected and performed under observation and performed without observation and performed during crises and performed during silence. The motion was back. The motion was the same. The motion had always been the same. The timer had never changed. The interval had never changed. The only thing that had changed was the room's relationship to the ringing, which had been, for a period, a thing that happened while other things were happening, and was now again the thing that the room was built around, the thing that the room paused for, the thing that the room nodded to.

The room nodded.

Austen sat across from me with his notepad. The notepad was the same notepad he had carried since the first meeting, the notepad that contained the minutes and the ledger, and the internal record that he maintained with the precision of a person who knows that the record is not for anyone else. The record is for the room. And the room does not read the record. The room is the record.

"Same time next week," he said.

He said it the way he always did, as a statement that was also a question, a promise, and a fact. At the same time next week, the room would be here. The pineapple would be here. The timer would ring. The ice would arrive. The puzzle would advance. The labels would multiply. The Psychoanalyst would analyze something that did not need analyzing. Byron would break something. Woolf would see something nobody else saw. Dickens would propose a project that involved everyone's surface area.

The Club would continue.

Not because the Club had a mission. Not because the Club had a grant or a board or a brochure or a statement of purpose or a program or a vision for the future. The Club would continue because the people in it would come back, and the coming back was the mission, and the mission was the coming back, and the two were the same thing and had always been the same thing and would always be the same thing.

"Same time next week," I said.

The egg timer ticked.

The pineapple presided.

The ice was good.

Poe spoke. Only I heard it. One word. The same word I've been carrying since the first invitation. Adequate. The dogs didn't stir. The pineapple didn't move. The room kept going. I wrote this down so I don't forget the sound of a raven finally agreeing with the floor.

Chapter 13

ADEQUATE

The room was quiet.

Not the quiet of an empty room. The quiet of a full one. The quiet of a room where every chair is occupied by the person who belongs in it, and every person is doing the thing they do, and the doing does not require commentary because the doing is the commentary.

Steinbeck was at my feet. His breathing was slow, steady, the breathing of a creature whose trust in the room was so complete that consciousness was optional. His paws twitched. He was dreaming. Dogs dream about the things they did during the day, which means Steinbeck was dreaming about lying on a floor and trusting people, which was the same thing he did when he was awake, which meant Steinbeck's dreams and Steinbeck's life were the same thing, and the sameness was either the simplest or the most profound form of contentment, and the distinction did not matter to Steinbeck, and the not mattering was the contentment.

Hemingway was across the room. He had taken a position. The position was near the door, but not at the door. The position had shifted by approximately two feet since the first meeting, which was the most Hemingway had ever adjusted his stance, and the adjustment was not a retreat and not an advance. It was a settling. Hemingway had spent months standing at the exact threshold between the room and the world, guarding the border, assessing every entry. The two-foot shift was Hemingway's way of saying that the border no longer required the same vigilance, not because the threats had ended but because the room had proven it could survive them, and a room that could survive its threats did not need a dog at the door. It needed a dog in the room. Hemingway was in the room. The room was better for it. Hemingway did not acknowledge the shift. Hemingway never acknowledged adjustments. Adjustments were made, and they were in the new position, which was defended with the same conviction as the old position, because conviction was not attached to the position. Conviction was attached to Hemingway.

Byron was asleep on the pineapple.

This should not have been possible. The pineapple was not shaped for sleeping. The pineapple had a crown of stiff, pointed leaves, an exterior of armored hexagonal segments, and a general architecture designed by evolution to discourage exactly the kind of contact that Byron was making. But Byron was asleep on it. Byron was draped across the top of the pineapple with the boneless, improbable comfort of a creature who has never once accepted that a surface is unsuitable, because suitability is a judgment, and Byron did not make judgments about surfaces. Byron made claims. The pineapple had been claimed. The claiming was complete. Byron's body rose and fell with his breathing, and the pineapple bore his weight with the same silent, immovable patience that the pineapple brought to everything, which was the patience of a thing that has outlasted every challenge by the simple method of not responding to any of them.

The pineapple was still dented. The dent from the fall had not healed because pineapples do not heal. Pineapples are not designed for recovery. Pineapples are designed for one sustained act of being, and the being includes whatever happens to them during the being, and what had happened to this pineapple was a fall and a rescue and a return, and the fall and the rescue and the return were now part of the pineapple's surface, visible, permanent, and unremarked upon, because the Club did not remark upon damage. The Club sat with damage. The Club's entire membership was composed of people and animals who had been dented by something and had continued presiding over their own lives without waiting for the dent to be fixed, because the dent was not a flaw. The dent was a record. And the record was the pineapple's way of saying what the Club had always said, which was: I was here. Something happened. I am still here.

Woolf was by the window. The light was coming in at the angle that the light came in at this time of day, the angle that made the curtain translucent and the dust visible and the room look like a room in a painting that had been painted by someone who understood that the subject of the painting was not the room but the light in the room, and the light in the room was not the light from the sun but the light from the people, and the light from the people was not visible to a camera or an inspector or a clipboard but was visible to Woolf, and Woolf was visible to it, and the mutual visibility was the thing that Woolf had been looking at since the first meeting and would look at until the last.

Her fluorescent light stood in the corner, unplugged, retired, labeled. It stood the way decommissioned things stand, with the dignity of an object that served a purpose and the peace of an object that no longer needs to.

Dickens was working on the puzzle. He had found a second corner piece. The finding had occurred quietly, without announcement, during a moment when no one was watching, which was unusual for Dickens because Dickens's discoveries were usually accompanied by a speech and a proposal for a subcommittee to oversee the implications of the discovery. But this discovery had been quiet. Dickens had found the piece and placed it and looked at it and nodded and continued working, and the quiet was new, and the new was good, and the good was the kind of good that does not announce itself because announcing itself would change it.

Twelve percent. Two corners confirmed. The barn was definitive. The sky was expanding. The green was connecting to something that might have been a fence, or might have been a road, or might have been the puzzle's way of saying that not everything needs to be identified to be placed.

Twain was at the table, label maker beside her, not labeling. She was sitting. She was sitting with the label maker within reach and not reaching for it, which was the Twain equivalent of meditation, the state of being in the proximity of one's instrument without using it, the trust that the instrument would be there when needed and the recognition that the needing was not constant, and the not-constant was not a failure of the labeling but a success of the room, because a room that is fully labeled is a room that has been fully observed, and a fully observed room does not need more observation. It needs presence. Twain was present. The label maker was present. The labels were on the walls, and the chairs and the timer, and the pineapple, and the labels were the room's memory of itself, and the memory was complete, and the completeness allowed Twain to sit.

She would label something before the meeting ended. She always did. But for now, she sat, and the sitting was enough.

Melville was holding his ice. Not a glass of ice. The bag. He was holding the bag the way he always held the bag, with both hands, against his chest, the cold pressing through the plastic into his shirt, and the cold was the reassurance, and the reassurance was the contact, and the contact was Melville's way of knowing that the ice was still ice and the still-ice was still his and the his was still the room's and the room was still the place that deserved the carrying.

The bag was full. The bag was cold. The bag was from the Sonic Drive-In on Fourth Street, the one near the overpass. Always the one near the overpass. The one near the mall had replaced their machine, and the new machine did not understand compression, and Melville did not forgive machines that did not understand compression, and the not forgiving was permanent, and the permanent was the principle, and the principle was Melville.

The Psychoanalyst was in his chair. The most comfortable chair. The chair he had claimed on the first day and returned to on every subsequent day with the gravitational inevitability of a body that has found its orbit and will not be displaced by argument or analysis or a dog sitting on its foot.

He was quiet. The quiet was not permanent. The quiet was the Psychoanalyst gathering observations the way a storm gathers moisture, slowly, invisibly, with the understanding that the gathering would eventually produce something, and the something would be delivered to the room whether the room wanted it or not, and the room would tolerate it because tolerating the Psychoanalyst was one of the Club's unwritten agreements, and the agreement was maintained not because the Psychoanalyst was right but because the Psychoanalyst was sincere, and sincerity, even misapplied sincerity, even sincerity that lands on you like an unwanted diagnosis, was the one quality the Club did not reject.

Hemingway was no longer sitting on his foot. Hemingway had moved to the room. The foot was free. The Psychoanalyst did not mention the freedom of the foot. The freedom was new, and the Psychoanalyst was processing the newness, and the processing would eventually become an observation about the dog's shifting boundaries as a metaphor for the Club's evolving relationship with external authority, and the observation would be delivered at the worst possible moment, and the moment would pass, and the room would continue.

Austen sat across from me with his notepad.

The notepad was open. The pen was in his hand. The pen had signed things that mattered and recorded things that mattered and written minutes that mattered, and the mattering was Austen's contribution and the contribution was invisible, and the invisibility was the point because the point of maintaining a room is not to be seen maintaining it. The point of maintaining a room is the room.

"Same time next week," he said.

It was not a question.

The egg timer rang.

The ring filled the room the way the ring always filled

the room, completely, briefly, and without explanation. The ring was the ring. The ring measured nothing. The ring meant everything. The ring was the Club's heartbeat, the mechanical pulse that said the room was alive and the alive was continuing, and the continuing was all the room had ever promised, and all the room had ever delivered, and the promise and the delivery were the same thing.

The room nodded.

Austen reset it.

The interval began.

The interval would end, and the timer would ring, and Austen would reset it, and the interval would begin again, and again, and again, and the again was not repetition. The again was the point. The again was the Club's answer to every question it had ever been asked, by the Department and the brochure and the survey and the grant and the board and the inspector and the renovation and the social media plan and the intergenerational panels and the programming and the chair yoga and the guided breathing and the creative prompts and the mission statement and the statement of purpose and every person who had ever walked into this room and asked "what is this for?"

The answer was: again. The room is for again. The pineapple presides again. The timer rings again. The ice arrives again. The puzzle advances again. The labels multiply again. The cat breaks something again. The raven watches again. The people come back again.

Again is the mission. Again is the vision. Again is the purpose. Again is the grant the Club awarded itself on the first day and renews every Thursday, and funds with nothing except the decision to return.

Poe was on the back of the sofa.

He had been on the back of the sofa for the entire

meeting, which was where he had been for every meeting since the inspection, having relocated from the curtain rod to a position that was lower, closer, and more integrated into the room. The relocation was three feet of altitude and a lifetime of proximity. Poe was no longer above the room. Poe was in the room. The raven had descended from observation to participation, and the participation was silent, and the silence was the participation.

He had been watching. He had always been watching. He had watched the letter arrive, and the brochure arrive, and the grant arrive, and the survey arrive, and the board form and the programming begin, and the inspector inspect, and the pineapple fall and the pineapple return and the vote happen and the grant decline and the room empty and the room fill, and the room become itself again. He had watched all of it from above, and now he watched it from among, and the watching was the same watching, and the watching was the only thing Poe had ever done, and the doing was enough.

Poe fluffed his feathers.

The fluffing was not casual. The fluffing was the kind of fluffing a bird does when the bird is preparing. Preparing for flight or preparing for stillness or preparing for the thing that comes after watching, which is speaking, and speaking is the thing Poe had not done, had almost done, had begun to do three times in the Club's history and stopped each time because the time was not the time.

The room did not notice. The room was doing what the room did. Dickens was placing a puzzle piece. Twain was reaching for the label maker because something had gone unlabeled for too long, and the too long was over. Melville was pouring ice. Woolf was watching the light. The Psychoanalyst was formulating something that no one had requested. Byron was asleep on the pineapple. Steinbeck was dreaming of floors. Hemingway was holding his new position with the permanence of a dog who has decided.

Austen was writing in the notepad.

I was in my chair.

The chair that had been through things.

Poe opened his beak.

The room did not stop. The room did not pause. The room continued being the room, which was the condition Poe had been waiting for, because Poe had not been waiting for silence. Poe had been waiting for the room to be so fully itself that one more sound would not change it, would not disrupt it, would not cause anyone to turn and stare and assign meaning to the sound. Poe had been waiting for the moment when speaking would be the same as not speaking, when the word would enter the room and the room would absorb it, the way the room absorbed everything, completely and without ceremony.

Poe tilted his head.

The throat moved. The chest expanded. The beak opened to its full extension, which was not wide but was deliberate, the deliberateness of a creature that has held a sound inside itself for a very long time and is now releasing it not because the sound needs to be heard but because the holding is finished.

And Poe said:

"Adequate."

The word was small. The word was dry. The word was delivered with the flat, unhurried precision of a creature that has considered every word in every language it has ever heard spoken in every room it has ever watched and has selected this one, this single word, as the word that says what needs to be said.

Not "nevermore." Not prophecy. Not drama. Not the dark, theatrical declaration that ravens are supposed to make in rooms where humans have gathered to be important. Not the literary gesture. Not the gothic flourish. Not the word that a raven in a poem would say.

The word that a raven in a room would say.

Adequate.

The room is adequate. The pineapple is adequate. The timer is adequate. The ice is adequate. The chairs are adequate. The people are adequate. The cat is adequate. The dog by the door is adequate. The dog on the floor is adequate. The labels are adequate. The puzzle is adequate. The light by the window is adequate. The light in the corner is adequate. The man who analyzes is adequate. The man who builds is adequate. The woman who labels is adequate. The woman who sees is adequate. The man who carries ice is adequate. The man who opens doors is adequate. The man who writes is adequate.

Adequate. Enough. Sufficient. The room works. The room has always worked. The room will continue to work. Not because the room is extraordinary. Not because the room is vibrant. Not because the room has a mission or a vision or a strategic plan or a brochure or a grant or a board of directors. Because the room is adequate. Because adequate is the highest praise a raven can give, because a raven has watched everything, and everything is mostly inadequate, and the things that are adequate are the things that work, and the things that work are the things that last, and the things that last are the things that a raven, after years of watching and waiting and holding the word inside its chest, finally considers worth the breath.

Adequate.

Poe folded his wings. He tucked his beak into his chest feathers. He closed his eyes.

He went to sleep.

Nobody heard him. Nobody in the room heard the word. The room was too busy being the room. Dickens was exclaiming softly about a puzzle piece. Twain was applying a label. Melville was pouring. Woolf was watching. The Psychoanalyst was beginning a sentence. Byron was dreaming on the pineapple. Steinbeck was dreaming on the floor. Hemingway was not dreaming. Hemingway was awake and holding his position because someone had to be awake, and Hemingway had decided it would be him.

Nobody heard the raven speak.

But I heard.

I was in my chair, the chair that had been through things, and I heard the word, and the word was enough, and enough was the word, and the word went to sleep, and the room continued, and the egg timer ticked, and the pineapple presided, and the ice was good.

Epilogue

The pineapple was replaced on a Tuesday.

Not because it had failed. Not because it had expired, though pineapples do expire, and this one had been presiding for longer than any pineapple in recorded history had been asked to preside, and the presiding had taken a toll that was visible in the softening of the skin and the browning of the crown and the general posture of a fruit that had held its position through a letter, a brochure, a survey, a grant application, a board of directors, an inspection, a renovation proposal, a social media campaign, a fall from the table, a rescue by a dog, and a vote that determined the future of the room it had governed without complaint.

The pineapple was replaced because Austen replaced it.

He did not announce the replacement. He did not convene a meeting. He did not consult the membership or the minutes or the egg timer. He arrived on a Tuesday, when the room was empty, and he removed the old pineapple from the table and placed a new pineapple in the same spot with the same alignment and the same quarter-inch distance from the egg timer.

The new pineapple was slightly larger. The new pineapple was slightly greener. The new pineapple had an unblemished surface, an upright crown, and the rigid, formal posture of a fruit that has not yet been through anything and does not know what is coming.

The old pineapple was not discarded. Austen took it home. What Austen did with it at home is not recorded in the minutes because the minutes cover proceedings at the Club, and Austen's home is not the Club, and the boundary between the two is the boundary that the Club respects, and the respect is maintained by the not-asking.

Nobody mentioned the replacement at the next meeting. Nobody looked at the new pineapple and said, "That is a new pineapple." Nobody compared the new pineapple to the old pineapple. Nobody mourned the old pineapple, or welcomed the new one, or asked whether the transition had been conducted according to proper governance, because there was no proper governance for pineapple succession. There was only Austen, and Austen had decided, and the deciding was the governance.

The new pineapple presided.

It presided the way the old pineapple had presided, which was by being in the center of the table and not explaining itself and not welcoming anyone and not symbolizing anything, and not participating in any conversation about what it meant or what it was for.

Byron circled it twice and sat beside it.

The egg timer rang.

The room nodded.

Austen reset it.

I tell you this because the question I am most frequently

asked about The Evergreen Club is whether it is real, and the answer is that the question is the wrong question. The right question is whether the room is real, and the answer to the right question is that every room where people come back is real, and every pineapple that presides without explanation is real, and every egg timer that measures nothing and means everything is real, and every dog that trusts the floor is real, and every dog that guards the door is real, and every cat that sleeps on a thing that was not designed for sleeping is real, and every raven that watches for years and says one word is real, and the one word is adequate, and adequate is real, and real is adequate, and the two words are the same word, and the same word is enough.

The Club meets on Thursdays. The door is open. Austen opens it before you knock.

The pineapple will not be explained.

You are welcome to inspect the chairs.

Same time next week.

About the Author

If the world were a more sensible place, authors would be sensible people who lived in sensible houses with sensible pets and wrote sensible books about sensible things. This, however, is not the case with Coyote Gray Sr, a retired rancher in central New Mexico whose general refusal to behave like a manageable person has produced consequences, some of them literary. His life is the sort that causes librarians to lock the biography section after dark and whisper warnings to small children, though The Evergreen Club is in fact his first book. He wrote it after proposing a bet to his son and grandson, and then being mule headed enough to see it through.

For permissions, inquiries, or correspondence:
Coyote Pack Publishing
info@coyotepackpublishing.com